REGENCY
CHARADE

REGENCY CHARADE

Margaret Mayhew

Walker and Company
New York

First published in the United States of America in 1986 by the
Walker Publishing Company, Inc.

Published simultaneously in Canada by John Wiley & Sons,
Canada, Limited, Rexdale, Ontario.

Library of Congress Cataloging-in-Publication Data

Mayhew, Margaret, 1936-
  Regency charade.

  I. Title.
PR6063.A887R44   1986   823'.914   86-9110
ISBN 0-8027-0912-5

Printed in the United States of America

10 9 8 7 6 5 4 3 2 1

REGENCY
CHARADE

=== 1 ===

THE YOUNG GENTLEMAN travelling alone in a hired coach towards the wilder parts of England was strikingly handsome. His style of dress proclaimed the dandy, and his features, impeccable breeding. From his fair hair, cut with studied carelessness into curls over his temples *à la* Brummell, to his shiny hussar boots propped comfortably on the seat opposite, he was every inch the man of fashion. He was also exceedingly drunk.

He had been dozing pleasantly for some time, his head lolling against the cushions behind him and his heavy-lidded eyes half-shut. The scenery had had little to offer of interest for the past ten miles; there had been nothing to see but bleak moorland and distant hills. Now it was growing dark. He fumbled for his cane and rapped clumsily on the roof above him. The coach slowed and drew to a halt and the gentleman, after some small difficulty, opened the door and stumbled out.

The icy wind hit him like a blow, whipping at the skirts of his coat and causing him to stagger slightly. After the warmth of the coach, the bitter cold had a sobering effect. He stood for a moment, and then shook his head as though to clear it: He had no recollection of what he was doing in the hired coach or where he was supposed to be going in this alien countryside.

The coachman, a rotund silhouette against the wide skies, peered down from his box with misgiving. The gentleman had been drunk since they had left London nearly six days ago, and although the driver had been well paid for his hire, he was heartily regretting it. There had been nothing but trouble from the first. At one inn there had been a sword fight, at another fisticuffs, and, at a third, an awkward incident where the gentleman had apparently insulted a lady whose husband had demanded satisfaction. Fortunately, his passenger had forestalled any such possibility by sliding beneath the table in a state of complete unconsciousness and having to be carried out to the coach. The coachman was dismayed to see him now on his feet again and to receive a sharp prod from the gentleman's cane.

"Down you get, there's a good fellow."

"D-down, sir?"

"That is what I just said. Are you deaf?"

"But the horses, sir . . ."

"Your pace is too slow for me, my friend. I will take the reins now. Give me your coat."

The coachman hesitated, hearing the slurred voice and seeing the tall figure sway a little like a reed in a gentle wind, but at another, yet sharper jab from the cane he made haste to climb down and to divest himself of his many-caped greatcoat, which the other donned, after some fumbling, over his own exquisitely cut one. The gentleman having proved all too clearly that he was a person it was not wise to cross, the coachman watched without protest as his passenger climbed up onto the box and took up the reins.

The gentleman looked down over his shoulder. "Since I have taken your place you may take mine—inside."

"Thank you, sir."

"Where are we going?"

The coachman stared. "Where, sir?"

"That is what I just asked you."

"Don't you remember, sir?"

"If I remembered, my good fellow," was the impatient reply, "I should not have asked you."

"We are going to Kielder Castle, sir."

"Are we? And how far are we from this castle?"

"It's three miles or more on from Alnwick, and that's a good twelve miles along this road. I doubt we'll make it before nightfall, sir."

The young gentleman smiled. "We shall see. We'll get fresh horses at the next post. What is the name of this godforsaken county, by the way?"

"Northumberland, sir."

"Northumberland! Why in heaven's name did you bring me here?"

"You asked me to, sir. All the way from London."

"Did I? Did I indeed? Wait a moment . . . Kielder Castle, you said?"

"That's right, sir."

The gentleman smiled again and spoke softly to himself. "I remember now. . . . Of course, *Kielder* . . ." He reached for the whip. "What are you standing there for, man? Inside, and quick about it, before I leave you behind."

The coachman hurriedly did as he was bid and sat himself gingerly on the edge of the cushioned seat. Hardly had he done so than the conveyance started forward with a jerk that hurled him backwards, his jackbooted feet in the air, his hat over his eyes. His fingers, clutching for a hold, closed round something hard on the seat beside him, and he saw that it was an empty brandy bottle. In disgust he tossed it into the corner and then clung for dear life to the strap as they careered at breakneck speed along the turnpike, the horses at full stretch. The coachman shut his eyes and began to pray, expecting to be overturned at any minute. This was a wild 'un, and no mistake—a real devil. He felt sorry for the people who lived at the castle, whoever they were . . .

While the coach with its hapless passenger raced on at

full pelt northwards, two people were sitting beside a fire in the great hall of Kielder Castle, absorbed in a game of chess and blissfully unaware that every turn of the wheels brought an uninvited visitor nearer to them. A brown and white spaniel slept contentedly at their feet, silky paws outstretched towards the blaze. A long-case clock ticked rhythmically in a corner, and candles, flickering in iron sconces, made shadows dance on the walls. The wind buffeted the old wooden shutters so that they creaked and groaned.

"Check!" said Sir William Spencer triumphantly, and looked across the table at his sister.

Miss Spencer considered the board calmly, and after only a moment's deliberation, removed her king to safety. Her brother frowned and chewed his lower lip, resting his chin on his hand so that his face was within a few inches of the pieces. His triumph had been short-lived, and it was several minutes before he made another move. His sister waited patiently. Sir William's hand hovered first over one piece, then another, and finished by tamely advancing a pawn one rank. In doing so he had unhappily exposed his queen, and he watched in indignation as the black bishop swooped to capture her.

"I say, Kate, I didn't mean you to do that."

"I know you did not. You must pay more attention, Will."

"I do pay attention," he protested. "But there's so much to think about all at once."

"Your move."

The baronet sighed and bent again to the task of trying to beat his sister—just once. He was nine years old and by no means a duffer, but Katherine always won at chess. In fact, she always seemed to win at everything, so far as he was concerned. Thirteen years his senior, she had had charge of him for as long as he could remember, ever since their mother had died soon after he was born, and their father, in his grief, had assumed the life of a semirecluse, scarcely leaving his room until he had followed his wife to the grave five years later. Sir William looked forward to the day when he would be big enough to do exactly as he pleased and tell his sister so; he also looked forward to the day when he would beat her at chess. Without much hope, or caution, he moved his knight. Miss Spencer promptly marched her queen sideways across the board.

"Checkmate."

And Sir William, with utter disgust, saw that it was.

Miss Spencer looked at the clock and began to put away the chess pieces in their black japanned box.

"I'm not going to bed yet," the baronet said quickly.

"Not yet," his sister agreed. "But soon. You are only just recovered from that chill."

"I wish you would not fuss me so much, Kate."

She smiled at him and ruffled his hair. "I don't fuss."

"You do, you do," he protested crossly, brushing her hand away. "You and Nurse treat me like a baby. But I'm not a baby anymore. I'm head of the family now. Since Harry was killed."

Miss Spencer put away the last chess piece in the box and shut the lid. "Certainly you are head of the family, Will," she agreed. "Kielder belongs to you now. And when you are come of age neither Nurse nor I nor anyone will have the right to interfere with what you choose to do. You will be able to go to bed just when you like and do as you please about everything. Until then, I must keep my promise to Mama to look after you and see you come to no harm."

"You are going to fuss for years and years," he groaned, "just because Harry killed himself in a silly race. You're afraid I shall be like him."

"Don't be nonsensical, Will. You are nothing whatever like Harry and never will be—thank goodness."

"*He* never did as you told him. He did just as he pleased. He didn't care."

"No," said Miss Spencer. "Harry didn't care, it is perfectly true. He didn't care for anything or anybody —and certainly not for Kielder, as he should have done."

Will said darkly, "When I come of age I think I shall go to London, like Harry."

"I hope you are not serious. Your duty is at Kielder. Never forget that it has belonged to our family for nearly five hundred years."

"You never let me forget it," he muttered. "I'm tired of hearing about it. So was Harry."

Miss Spencer stood up, the chess box cradled in her arms. "Don't take Harry for your model, Will," she said softly. "Be proud of Kielder. You should be. See that it passes to your son and to your son's son, and there will be Spencers here for hundreds more years."

Will, who could not see beyond the next day, did not answer but hunched his shoulders rebelliously. His sister said no more, and went to put away the chess box and board in the oak armoire that stood against the wall. She was tall and rather thin, with very fine brown eyes and dark hair drawn back from a wide brow into a simple chignon. She moved gracefully and carried herself well. There was a pride in her bearing—the family pride which she had admonished her young brother for lacking. It compensated for her want of true beauty, and disguised the fact that she was very shabbily dressed in a mourning gown that was many years old and had been outmoded when first made by a local seamstress. She wore no jewellery except for a small gold and amethyst brooch which had once belonged to her mother.

The great hall mirrored this state of affairs. There were only a few pieces of furniture, although these were lovingly cared for, and the upholstery on the settee and chairs should have been replaced years ago. There was an unmistakable air of dignified poverty. Nothing, however, could detract from the fine proportions of the hall, the splendour of the high beamed ceiling, the mellowness of the stone walls, and the grandeur of the big stone fireplace with the Spencer arms engraved above. At the opposite end of the hall a wide oak staircase rose to a galleried landing, where minstrels had once played for the Spencers of long ago. Kielder Castle had been given to the family by King Edward III in 1332 as payment against expenses incurred by them in helping the King defend the North of England against the Scots. From a fortress it had become a home, and generations of the family had been born and grown up within its dour grey walls. The fourteenth baronet, who with his dark hair and dark eyes bore a strong resemblance not only to his sister but also to several of the portraits of his ancestors that hung upon the walls, now sat scuffing at a hole in the carpet with the toe of his shoe.

Katherine Spencer drew her shawl closer round her shoulders and encouraged the fire a little with the aid of a poker and a pair of bellows, both so large and heavy she could scarcely lift them. Despite screens placed at strategic points, the hall was very cold. Although Miss Spencer would not have admitted it, the castle was draughty and appallingly uncomfortable to live in. She was debating with herself whether to indulge in the extravagance of more wood on the dwindling fire when the butler, Purves, entered from a door beside the staircase. This door led to another stairway, which descended to the ground floor, the great hall being on the first floor of the castle. In olden times a flight of stone steps had mounted the outside, giving directly through an arched doorway into the hall, but these steps had long since crumbled away and the doorway had been blocked up, leaving only the trace of the archway visible. The main entrance to Kielder was now at ground level.

The butler appeared flustered. He was elderly and frail and unaccustomed to anything untoward disturbing the daily routine.

"A gentleman has arrived, ma'am. He wishes to speak with you."

"A gentleman, Purves? At this hour? What does he want?"

The butler could not say. The gentleman's name was Mr. Drew—that was all the information he had been given.

Miss Spencer was equally perplexed and uncertain. The name meant nothing to her, but it was not unknown for travellers in difficulties to ask for help, and naturally, this was never refused.

"Has this gentleman's carriage broken down, Purves? Is he in need of assistance?"

"He did not say no, ma'am. The coach appeared to be in good order." The butler paused, and then added in puzzled tones, "The gentleman was driving it himself, whilst his coachman rode inside. I—I made the unfortunate error, ma'am, of mistaking one for the other—just at first, until I could see them better and the gentleman spoke."

Will began to laugh, but his sister quelled him with a look. She understood how distressed Purves would have been at making such a mistake. He had always prided himself on devoted service and perfection in his work and now, with shaky hands, failing eyesight and health, and a mere handful of staff under his direction, he struggled to maintain old standards. Ten years ago he would never have confused a coachman and a gentleman, no matter how they had travelled.

"Do you think I should see this Mr. Drew, Purves?"

The butler hesitated. "He appears to be a gentleman of some standing, ma'am, to judge by his manner and appearance. And he asked for you by name."

"Then you had better show him up."

The butler inclined his head gravely and withdrew.

"What does he want, Kate? Who is he?"

"How should I know, Will? We must wait and see.

Stand up and be ready to make your bow as I have taught you. We must show Mr. Drew some courtesy—whoever he may be."

The advent of a stranger at the castle was not unwelcome. They saw few people except for a small circle of neighbours, the nearest of whom lived five miles away. Brother and sister waited, wondering, and even the brown and white spaniel, who had been lazily snoring away in front of the fire all this while, lurched to his feet and looked expectant.

When Mr. Drew entered the great hall Miss Spencer's first feeling was of great astonishment. She had anticipated someone middle-aged, but the man who appeared was only a year or two older than herself. It was not only his youth that took her aback but also his looks: he was, without doubt, the handsomest man she had ever seen in her life. And he was also the most elegant. Her brother Harry had fancied himself as a follower of fashion, and had affected all kinds of extremes of dress that she had privately thought ridiculous. Now Katherine saw and recognised the restraint of true elegance. The square-cut tailcoat which he wore had been superbly tailored without the need for resort to any fancy or vulgar embellishment, and the close-fitting pantaloons were worn inside hussar boots that, despite being well-specked with mud, were clearly of the first style and quality. She received the impression that whereas Harry had been forever rearranging his cravat and fretting over the life of his shirt collar, this gentleman, once these things had been donned, would pay them no more attention.

She curtsied. As Mr. Drew approached and bowed to her, she saw her own surprise reflected for a moment in his blue eyes. If I expected someone quite different, she thought, then so did he. She saw, too, that in one respect, at least, he resembled her late brother: he was rather the worse for drink.

Will was presented and managed a creditable bow.

Boots, the spaniel—so named because of the brown markings on all four paws—padded forward, wagging his feathery tail politely, and received a casual pat. Refreshment was offered and accepted and Miss Spencer invited their visitor to sit beside the fire. She seated herself, and Will perched on a small oak stool and watched the stranger with lively curiosity. Boots lay down and went to sleep again.

Mr. Drew appeared completely at ease. He put up his eyeglass and inspected the great hall carefully, leaning back to study the beamed ceiling.

"So this is Harry's ruin," he remarked after a minute or two.

Miss Spencer drew a breath. Already alerted against the visitor by reason of his overindulgence, she was now doubly on her guard. She made up her mind then and there that she did not like Mr. Drew. Despite his good looks and elegance, there was a careless conceit about him that irked her, and his unflattering reference to Kielder clinched the matter. She regarded him coldly.

"You were acquainted with my brother, sir?"

Mr. Drew lowered his glass and smiled suddenly at her. If he had been handsome in repose, the effect when he smiled was devastating: the corners of his eyes crinkled most attractively, and his teeth were very white and even. Miss Spencer, however, was immune.

"I knew Harry, yes. I would offer you my condolences, Miss Spencer, on his untimely death, were it not for the fact that it can only be a relief to you to be rid of so tiresome and prodigal a brother." He raised his glass again and looked at Will briefly. "The new baronet appears to me to promise far better."

She could hardly believe her ears. However much the sentiments he had expressed accorded with her innermost feelings, she was not even prepared to admit it to herself, let alone to a complete stranger.

"You are not aware perhaps, sir, that my late brother

was buried only five days ago, but had he been dead for as many years I should not wish to hear ill spoken of him."

Mr. Drew did not appear in the least embarrassed by this tart rejoinder. "I admire the way you leap to Harry's defence, Miss Spencer. It is far more than he deserved. He would not, I fear, have been so ready to leap to yours."

Again, this was painfully near the real truth of the matter, but Katherine was spared from the need to reply by the entrance of Purves with a tray set with decanters and glasses. Mr. Drew accepted a glass of brandy, whilst Miss Spencer took a small glass of canary wine. This all took some time to accomplish, as the old butler moved very slowly, and by the time he had withdrawn Katherine had decided to come straight to the point.

"May we know the purpose of your calling here, sir? I collect it has something to do with my late brother?"

"Oh yes, it has something to do with Harry," Mr. Drew said, admiring the contents of his glass. "This is a very passable cognac, Miss Spencer."

She said coolly, "My father kept an excellent cellar; some of it still remains to us."

"You surprise me. I should have thought Harry would have drunk it dry."

That there was a single bottle left in the cellar was only due to the fact that Harry had gone to live in London for the final year of his life, but Miss Spencer had no intention of confessing this to Mr. Drew, whom she liked less and less with every passing minute. The intelligence that her brother had apparently continued his drinking habits in London came as no surprise to her: she had resigned herself long ago to the knowledge that Harry would never change. He was weak, vain, and foolish, and thus he had remained until the day he had died overturning his curricle in a senseless race between London and Brighton.

11

She could remember vividly the awful scene when Harry, flushed and furious, had shouted at her that he was going to leave Kielder forever. He hated the place! He *loathed* it! It was nothing but a ramshackle ruin! And he was bored to death with living in the wilds. He wanted to enjoy himself, for once—to spend his money on something other than leaking roofs and rotting gutters. He was going to spend it instead on decent clothes, on horses, on good food and wine—on all the things that made life worth living. And he was going to do so in company with the *ton* and not with a lot of dull, dreary provincials. In short, he was going to London. She was welcome to spend the rest of *her* life scrimping and scraping to keep Kielder from falling down, if that was what she wanted, but he was not staying another day. . . .

Katherine looked at Mr. Drew. If Harry had passed his time in company with such people, it was little wonder that he had gone from bad to worse. All her instincts warned her against this handsome, smiling stranger, with his elegant manner and impertinent remarks. She distrusted him deeply and disliked him even more. Will, however, had no such qualms. He piped up in friendly fashion.

"Did *you* take part in the race, sir—the one in which Harry was killed?"

Mr. Drew turned towards the boy. "Yes, I did."

"Harry always liked to drive very fast," Will continued. "He used to do from Alwick to Kielder in fifteen minutes."

"A trifle dilatory of him. But he was always mutton-fisted. I did it in twelve just now."

Will's eyes shone. "Did you really, sir? How famous! You must be a first-rate whip. Did you win the London-to-Brighton race?"

"I did."

"What were you driving, sir?"

"A curricle-and-four."

"Your own horses?"

"Naturally."

"Matched?"

"Chestnuts."

Will beamed with pleasure at the thought. "And how long did you take, sir?"

"Four hours, forty minutes."

"Is that the fastest time ever?"

"No. Not quite. The Regent has done it in ten minutes less."

"The *Regent*! Do you know him, sir? Have you—"

But Miss Spencer, who had had enough of this exchange, cut her brother short. He was young enough to be impressed by such exploits, and the spectre of him following in Harry's footsteps was ever in her mind. She added *insufferable conceit* to the growing list of their visitor's shortcomings, and prepared to remove her brother to safety.

"William, it is your bedtime now. You must make your bow to Mr. Drew."

But her brother was not going to give in without a struggle. "It's *not* time yet, Kate. Look at the clock. I want to stay. I want to talk to Mr. Drew."

"Then you cannot."

"But I want to."

"William, do as I say!"

Mr. Drew seemed amused by this interchange. He said languidly, "Sir William would be advised to stay, Miss Spencer. What I have to tell you concerns him equally."

Katherine hesitated. The sooner they learned the reason for this unwelcome visit, the sooner Mr. Drew would be gone and the happier she would be. She was obliged to offer him hospitality for the night, but she could not remember when she had taken against someone so vehemently and so instantly. And what was his purpose in coming all the way from London? Almost certainly Harry must have owed him money, as he had owed so many others, and he had come to reclaim the debt from the estate. Unless it was a small sum—and nothing could be less likely—then she would be in the humiliating position of being unable to repay it. She drew herself up in her chair.

"Will you tell us now why you are here, sir?"

He looked at her, letting his gaze wander slowly over her with what she considered monstrous insolence. To her annoyance, she felt herself blushing. It was a dreadful thought that he might perhaps mistake this for embarrassment or, worse still, gratification on her part. Well, let him stare! Much good might it do him! He need not fancy it would move her to anything but contempt and dislike.

Mr. Drew smiled, as though he read her thoughts. "You are younger than your brother Harry would have everyone believe. He made you out an old maid."

"Did he *really*?"

"Did he make her out a fusspot?" enquired Will with interest. "Because it's true. She does fuss, you know. All the time."

"Be quiet, Will."

"She was always trying to get Harry to do things he didn't want to do," Will went on, unabashed by the furious look his sister had given him. "I think that's partly why he went to London. To get away from Kate."

"*Will!*"

Miss Spencer was by now very pink in the face. She could imagine all too easily how Harry would have described her to his London friends. Only one year separated them, but it might as well have been ten. She had always felt many years older than Harry. Duties and decisions had somehow always fallen to her lot rather than to his, and Harry had been left free to pursue his own pleasure. He had resented any interference in this.

Many times she had tried to persuade him to shoulder some share of the burden, seeing that he was the heir, but Harry cared nothing for Kielder or for his family. He cared only for himself. Whatever he had said of her, it would certainly not be flattering.

"The only thing we need discuss with Mr. Drew is why he is here," she told Will. "*If* he will be good enough to tell us."

Their visitor set down his empty glass, and Sir William, with uncustomary helpfulness, hastened to refill it from the decanter. The glass, replenished to the brim, was returned to Mr. Drew under Miss Spencer's frosty eye. He raised it to her in a mock toast and drank.

"I will certainly tell you, Miss Spencer. But I am afraid you will not like what you hear. I am what I believe is commonly called the bearer of bad tidings."

Katherine's heart sank. It was going to be even worse than she had thought: thousands of pounds owed, not hundreds. If so, her legacy from Papa would have to be used to repay it, and that would leave them with almost nothing.

"I am ready to hear them, Mr. Drew," she said.

"Very well. I told you, Miss Spencer, that I knew your brother, Harry. We were not well acquainted but frequented the same places in London on occasion. White's, for instance."

"White's?"

"A gentlemen's club known especially for—er, its late-night gambling."

Katherine felt a shiver of fear. If Harry had started gaming in London, heaven alone knew how much he might have lost to someone like Mr. Drew, who probably spent most of his time in such clubs. Her brother had had no head for cards, but she could imagine him an easy victim of gamester's fever. It would have provided just the sort of excitement he craved and the recklessness he thrived on. No wonder all his modest inheritance had gone. What had not been spent on his fine new clothes and lavish living had evidently been lost at the tables.

Mr. Drew, who had been watching her, went on. "Your brother was in White's the night before he died— and so was I. I held the bank at the faro table where Harry was playing. He began to lose heavily, as he often did. He might have stopped, but unfortunately he had been drinking more than is wise at such times."

"In *your* experience, Mr. Drew?"

He smiled. "In my experience, Miss Spencer. Drinking and gambling make disastrous companions. I try to avoid the two meeting, whenever I remember. Your brother had not learned that lesson. And he began to bet on tick."

"On tick?"

"He was writing vowels, Miss Spencer. Notes of hand in place of money, and giving them to the bank."

"I see," she said. "Go on, please."

"There was some kind of argument, as I recall. I do not remember the precise details, but someone at the table made a remark in Harry's hearing about him. He took offence. The—er, inference of the remark was that he would not be able to redeem his vowels. He became very angry, and seemed to feel it necessary to prove it otherwise."

Miss Spencer had a sudden and ominous vision of Harry drunk and dishevelled at the gaming table, belligerently denying what she knew would probably have been the truth. The mockery and contempt of the fashionable around him would have stung very deep, he would have done anything to try and restore his credit. And Mr. Drew had presided over all this.

"What happened then?" she asked steadily.

"He staked Kielder Castle and all its lands," he said softly.

Katherine felt as though she were going to faint, or at least be very sick. "*Kielder!* Oh, he could not have done that! Even Harry could not have done that!"

"I assure you that he did. I have the proof of it here."

Mr. Drew took from his waistcoat pocket a crumpled piece of paper and held it out to her. "Here is your brother's vowel, Miss Spencer."

She stared at the paper with its untidy, blot-marked scrawl. It was Harry's hand and Harry's signature plain enough, she knew his odd way of fashioning his letters too well to doubt it, and, as usual, he had misspelled a word. And he had pledged Kielder—Kielder, which had belonged to the Spencers for hundreds of years—all for a moment of drunken vanity. The full implication of what her brother had done was dawning on her. She lifted her head.

"If you still hold this vowel, Mr. Drew, it must mean . . . it must mean—"

"It means that your brother lost his stake."

"Then you . . . *you* are the owner of Kielder!"

"That is so," he agreed.

Will jumped up from his stool. "You mean Kielder doesn't belong to me anymore? Is that true, Kate? Harry gambled it away?"

He looked bewildered rather than upset. Katherine went instantly to his side and put her arm about his shoulders.

"I'm afraid it *is* true, Will. The vowel is in Harry's hand. I could not mistake it. It—it is *infamous*! Such things should not be permitted! It is wicked beyond belief!" She turned on Mr. Drew, trembling with indignation and distress. "Sir, you have admitted that my brother was drunk at the time of making this wager. He was in no fit state to know what he was doing. Surely you should have torn up that piece of paper!"

"And insulted your brother still further by doing so? Tut, tut! My dear Miss Spencer, you do not appear to understand at all. A gambling debt is a debt of honour. I should have done Harry no service had I returned his vowel. Besides, he did not appear particularly out of countenance at losing something which he frequently

17

described as little better than a ruin. In fact, I should almost have said he was relieved to be rid of it. So relieved that the very next morning, before the race, he instructed his lawyers in London to hand over the deeds to me. They are already in my possession."

Katherine could well believe this. Her bitterness against her brother was so great at that moment that had he not been already dead and buried in the castle chapel, she felt she could have easily gone for him herself with any one of the rusting, ancient weapons that decorated the walls at Kielder. To have lost her beloved Kielder . . . and to a man like Mr. Drew! How could he! Oh, how *could* he!

"What are we going to do, Kate?" Will asked with interest. "Shall we have to leave Kielder?"

"That will not be necessary—for the moment, at any rate," Mr. Drew said lazily. "I am not proposing to turn you both out onto the moors, if that is what you are imagining."

He stretched his legs towards the fire and held out his empty glass to Will, who once again hurried to refill it from the decanter. Miss Spencer remained silent. She was casting about in her mind for a suitably dignified response but found herself quite unable to express any gratitude whatever for not being turned out of her own home. More trenchant replies were forming on her lips, but before she could utter any of them there was a *clump-clump* from the staircase, and she looked up to see Nurse descending, one step at a time, with remorseless and eager determination.

Nurse had looked after three generations of Spencers, and was as much a part of Kielder Castle as its walls. She was Scots—small, round as a haggis, and despite her advanced years, as canny as ever. Only her arthritic joints had obliged her to slow her pace and forced her to walk everywhere with a stick. Her long service had given her a privileged position in the family, which she used shamelessly. She reached the foot of the stairs and advanced into the centre of the great hall, where she stopped to survey the group beside the fireplace. When she spoke it was with a strong Scots accent.

"So—we've a visitor. And no one told me. What's to do?"

Mr. Drew put down his glass and rose to his feet. He made a low bow to the old woman, as though she were royalty, and Nurse was delighted. Her old eyes sparkled with appreciation, and she shuffled forward with surprising rapidity.

"I see someone's taught *you* your manners well, whoever you are. The same couldn't be said for most of the young today. Not to my way of thinking." She cocked a bright eye at Miss Spencer. "Well, who is he? Aren't you going to tell me?"

"This gentleman—" said Katherine in bitter tones, "this gentleman is Mr. Drew, the new owner of Kielder."

Nurse raised her eyebrows. "New owner of Kielder? What are you blethering about? What's been happening?"

Katherine explained in a low voice.

"Don't whisper—I canna hear a word. What's that you're saying?" The old woman bent her head closer. "Ha! Just what I'd've expected of Master Harry. He was always the rotten apple in the barrel. I knew it from the day he was born. You can tell. Aye, you can tell." She nodded sagely. "So . . . this fine, handsome young gentleman owns Kielder now?"

Mr. Drew smiled and bowed again.

"And a good thing too," Nurse declared roundly.

This was the final straw for Miss Spencer. "How can you say such a thing, Nurse! Don't you understand? Kielder will no longer belong to the family. Will is denied his rightful inheritance."

"Och, I understand all right," she replied calmly. "I'm not the old fool you take me for, missy. I say it's a *good* thing because at last you'll be rid of a millstone from around your necks."

"A *millstone*! *Kielder?*"

"Aye, that's what I said. It's falling to pieces—has been for years, ever since the family fortune went the way of the wind. And now Master Harry's spent what was left and all you have is a pile of debts and an old ruin."

"That's not so, Nurse," said Katherine, her voice low and vehement. "Kielder may need some repairs, but Will and I still have our legacies from Father."

"And precious little *that* was," Nurse snapped. "You'd've poured it all away, keeping this place just standing, stone on stone. As it is, thanks to this gentleman, you won't be able to. You'd do better to find a smaller home, you and Master William—one with a proper roof and windows."

"I don't want another home," she said quietly. "Kielder is my home. It has been our home for—"

"Five hundred years," the old woman interrupted. "Aye, I know all about that. And what of it? Come now, lassie, have some sense." She laid her hand on Katherine's arm and said more softly, " 'Tis best for Kielder—canna you see that? This Mr. Drew looks to me as though his pockets are well lined. He'll be able to take care of the old place better than you could. Think of that."

Miss Spencer could not bear to think of it, but nor did she wish to continue this conversation in front of Mr. Drew. The clock striking its silvery chimes from the corner intervened fortuitously to remind Nurse that it was William's bedtime. And nothing—storm, flood, tempest, or earthquake would have been permitted to interfere with the routine prescribed for her charge.

"Come on, Master William. High time you were abed." She looked at Katherine reproachfully. "The wee bairn looks tired out. He should never have left his bed so soon after that chill. Mark my words, it'll go on his chest again, just as before. And then where shall we be?"

Scolding and clucking like an old hen, she marshalled a furious Will towards the stairs and prodded him on upwards with her stick. The baronet's protests and the nurse's retorts could be heard for some time, until they faded away in the upper regions of the castle. Then there was silence.

"A remarkable woman," Mr. Drew said. "There is nothing so tyrannical as an old servant. My nurse is just the same. She rules us all still with a rod of iron."

Miss Spencer could imagine him as a child: willful and thoroughly spoiled for his good looks.

"You appear to me to be quite accustomed to having your own way, Mr. Drew," she said.

"Appearances can be deceptive," he replied, smiling.

She sat down again, and Boots thumped his tail sleepily at her feet. Katherine felt irrationally vexed that the spaniel should be so calm and content when such a calamity had occurred in their lives; Boots simply did not care—so long as there was a fire to lie beside and food in his bowl every day. Nurse did not seem to care, either, and even Will could not be said to be unduly upset. Nobody but herself truly appreciated the tragedy, the dreadful disaster of losing Kielder.

Mr. Drew had seated himself, too, crossing one leg casually over the other. He took a gold snuffbox from his waistcoat pocket, flicked open the lid, and took a pinch of the contents, inhaling carefully. He seemed completely at ease and quite unmoved by the situation—in fact, Miss Spencer formed the impression that he was enjoying himself immensely. She had not thought it possible to dislike anyone as much as she disliked him at that moment. As she stared at him, he looked up into her eyes so suddenly and directly that she was obliged to turn her own away.

"Don't distress yourself too much, Miss Spencer," he said. "Your nurse may be right. It might be better for Kielder."

Her anger flared suddenly and violently. "How can it

be! You know *nothing* about it, Mr. Drew! Nothing at all! This castle has belonged to my family since thirteen thirty-two. It was given to us by King Edward the Third. Spencers have lived and died here ever since. Five hundred years! And you say I should not be distressed! How would you feel, I wonder, Mr. Drew!"

He snapped the snuffbox lid shut. "How would you expect me to feel, Miss Spencer?"

She looked at him witheringly. "I am not sure I should expect you to feel very much. I am not sure you have any feelings at all. Do you own a family home of your own, Mr. Drew?"

"There are two in our family."

"Two! Then you can hardly have need of a third."

"They are both in the South. One in London and the other in the country. The idea of a property in the far-flung North rather appeals to me."

"But Kielder is very remote," she said. "You can have no idea what it is really like. The countryside is very wild, and in bad winters we are snowed in for weeks on end. Even in summer it is cold. I am persuaded *you* would not care for it at all. It would be very dull and uncomfortable for one accustomed to life in the South."

"Do you know, I think I should find the contrast rather refreshing," he replied. "A surfeit of Society and civilisation can jade the appetite. It can be very tedious. Very tedious indeed. Besides, I hear that the hunting and shooting are excellent in Northumberland."

"Oh, no," she said quickly. "Not at all. The hunting hereabouts is very poor—the land is too rough, and there are too many walls. As for the shooting, Harry always complained of the bag."

He smiled at her in his maddening way. "It is no use whatever trying to put me off, Miss Spencer. Are you hoping that I shall give up Kielder and go tamely back to London? Is that what you want?"

She met his eyes directly. "I want you to sell Kielder back to me, Mr. Drew."

He drained his glass; the heavy gold signet ring he wore on his left hand glinted in the firelight. "Can you afford to buy it?"

"That depends on your price," she said stiffly. "I am not entirely without means . . . there is a legacy from my father—"

He burst out laughing, and Katherine stared at him, outraged. It occurred to her then that he was far more drunk than she had supposed: his eyes shone with devilment.

"You would do almost anything to get Kielder back, wouldn't you?" he mocked. "Spend every penny you possess to keep it in the family for another five hundred years—even if it falls down within fifty."

"I want it back, yes."

"Then," he said smiling, as though to himself, "you will have to make yourself much more agreeable."

"What do you mean?"

He laughed again. "I mean that I shall be far more likely to sell Kielder back to you if you treat me better than you treated Harry."

He went to refill his glass from the decanter on the sideboard and returned to the fireplace, where he stood leaning his shoulders against the stone arch.

"Your severity, your sourness of temperament, your obstinate pride, your prudishness are all well known to me, I assure you," he continued pleasantly. "You are a positive virago, a shrew, a vixen . . . your brother told me so many times. I quite expected to have boiling oil poured over me from the battlements—but doubtless that will come. If you want Kielder back you will really have to try and behave very much better."

He was not only drunk but deranged as well, she decided. How dare he! How dare he speak so! Mr. Drew, unconcerned, rubbed the toe of one foot casually against Boots's fat stomach, and the dog rolled over on his back and waved his silky paws in the air, grunting his pleasure. At that moment, Miss Spencer would willingly have exchanged her beloved spaniel for an ill-tempered hound who might have had the good sense to bite that gentleman's ankle.

She rose to her feet and took up a candle. "I do not think any purpose can be served by discussing things further tonight. If you ring for Purves he will see to your needs."

He looked up from the dog and smiled; his blue eyes mocked. "You are afraid of me, Miss Spencer! Afraid to stay!"

"Certainly not," she retorted. "But I *am* afraid that the brandy has come between you and any reason."

"By God, Harry must have found you an uncomfortable sister! Did you read him lectures all the time?"

She did not deign to answer but made to pass him. As she did so, he grasped her arm tightly and twisted her towards him. She was tall enough for her face to be close to his, but she met his eyes without flinching. She could smell the brandy strong on his breath.

"Miss Straightlaced Spencer," he said mockingly. "I can see you are not afraid. But you should be—"

"Your cravat is burning, sir."

He looked down and gave a violent exclamation. The candle she held had caught the white folds of linen; at that moment the smouldering cloth burst into flame. He leapt back hastily, beating at his chest with his hands. The fire was put out, but the fine neckcloth was ruined, burned and blackened beyond repair. Mr. Drew lifted his head slowly.

"Did you do that on purpose, Miss Spencer?"

"Of course not, Mr. Drew."

"I do not believe you."

"As you please, sir."

He brushed at the singed linen. "I do not please. Very little about you pleases me so far, Miss Spencer. You are altogether too forceful for my tastes. I prefer more docile, amenable women."

"That is unfortunate for you."

"On the contrary, it is fortunate for *you*. Do you wish to pass?"

"If I may be permitted," she said with cold irony.

He moved a little to one side and held out his hand. "Good night then."

She hesitated a moment, not liking the look in his eye. When she allowed him to take her hand, he kissed it with exaggerated deference, at arm's length, and then when she was off her guard, jerked her suddenly against him and kissed her.

He released her almost at once with the taste of brandy on her lips. Katherine was so angry that she raised her hand to strike him. In the midst of her fury, however, she realised that to do so might only invite further insult and that if she wished to save Kielder from this man she must play her cards with the utmost caution and skill. She let her hand fall.

"That was dishonourable, Mr. Drew."

"I *am* dishonourable, Miss Spencer."

She retreated gingerly, but he made no further attempt to detain her. She ascended the stairs at a slow and dignified pace, turning once to look back. He was watching her, and raised his glass in salute again. She heard him laugh softly to himself. She had reached the gallery before she realised that Boots had remained traitorously below.

= 2 =

WHEN MISS LORRIMER of Langley Grange called the following morning she found her friend and neighbour, Miss Spencer, seated at her writing desk in a small room off the great hall, which served as a morning parlour. The Grange was five miles distant, but Miss Lorrimer, who had very little to do all day, was a frequent visitor at Kielder. The only child of an indulgent, if cantankerous, widowed father, she had no companions at home of her own age and, being of a warm and gregarious nature, found this a sore loss. Mr. Lorrimer was a semi-invalid and never left the grange; his daughter might have been presumed to lack no invitations except for the strong rumour in the county that the family's wealth was based on Trade. This naturally rendered Miss Lorrimer, despite being sole heiress to a substantial fortune, far less desirable: many a mama scouring the county for a suitable wife for her wellborn son had, regretfully, been obliged to pass her over. Miss Lorrimer, however, was not of the temperament which allows such things to put one in the dismals—at least, not for very long. She was nearly always cheerful, and this morning was no exception. She swept into the parlour all smiles, a plump little figure gowned in blue velvet with a bonnet to match that was trimmed with feathers and ribbon.

"Good morning, Kate. What are you doing frowning at your desk like that? It looks very strange."

Katherine roused herself from her reverie to greet her friend. "I'm very glad to see you, Letty."

"I should hope you are! Otherwise, I shall go away again at once. Or I would do, if I hadn't a surprise for you."

"A surprise?"

"Yes. Look!"

Miss Lorrimer untied the ribbon beneath her chin and with a grand flourish removed her bonnet. Beneath it, her previously ringleted fair curls had been transformed into a short, spiky cap that resembled a battered hedgehog. Miss Spencer gasped in horror.

"But Letty, your lovely curls . . ."

"Oh, pooh to them! I hated them. They were so old-fashioned." Miss Lorrimer revolved under Katherine's appalled gaze. "This is *à la* Titus. Everyone is wearing their hair like this in London. It said so in *The Ladies Toilette*, and my maid copied the picture for me. Isn't it fun? Don't you think so? I warned you I was going to try something *quite* different."

"Yes, but—"

"I can see you disapprove," Miss Lorrimer said, undismayed. "It may look a trifle *odd* to you at first, but I promise, you will become used to it. It is the very latest thing. All the crack!"

Miss Spencer smiled. Letty's passionate interest in the latest London fashions was fed entirely through magazines, which she devoured voraciously. She had never been further south than Newcastle, and nowhere near the capital, despite frequent invitations from an aunt to visit her there. Mr. Lorrimer approved of neither the aunt nor of London, and still less of his beloved only child leaving him to go so far away. And so, Letty's ambition to see at first hand all those things which she knew only as pictures in magazines had remained unfulfilled.

"If it is all the crack in London, Letty, then it must be

all right. I'm sure I shall become more used to it—in time. But whatever has your papa said?"

"Oh, he hasn't seen it yet. I dare say he will be furious and I shall be on bread and water for a week, but it will be worth it." Letty laughed. "At least I have made you smile, which is one good thing. I never saw you in such miseries. What are all those papers that you keep staring at?"

"Bills."

"Bills?"

Miss Lorrimer moved a little closer to the desk, bonnet in hand, and looked at the offending pile, perplexed. She had scarcely ever set eyes on a bill; her father saw to all such inconveniences of life. "You mean all those pieces of paper have to be *paid*?"

"That is usually the custom."

"But can't you just burn them or something, Kate? It must be very depressing to have to look at them all the time. No wonder you were looking so glum!"

"My dear Letty, what would be the use of that? If I burned them they would only send more."

"Then you must pay them and be rid of them, once and for all."

Katherine laughed. "Oh, Letty, you are incorrigible! But, of course, you are quite right. I *must* pay them . . . somehow. It's just that I really do not know where to start, or where the money is to come from. Will's legacy must not be touched, so it will have to come from mine— except that I may need it all . . ." She frowned thought-fully. "I suppose I could sell one of the paintings, but I don't think those we have left are worth very much— certainly not enough to pay all these bills that Harry left."

"They are all Harry's?"

"He left debts everywhere, Letty." Miss Spencer sighed. "It seems there is hardly a tailor or vintner in London to whom Harry did not owe something." She picked up one of the pieces of paper. "Listen to this: 'to blue cloth coat and waistcoat with silver buttons, lined complete, five pounds and twelve shillings.' That seems a very great deal to me."

"Not in London, Kate," Miss Lorrimer informed her kindly from her superior knowledge. "Who is the tailor?"

"A . . . a Mr. Weston of Bond Street."

"Well, *there* you are then."

"What do you mean, there I am?"

"Only that Mr. *Weston* is one of the very best tailors in London. Beau Brummell goes to him, and *all* the dandies! Have you *never* heard of him, Kate?"

"No, I have not. I might have known, though, that Harry would go to the most expensive."

"Imagine that," Miss Lorrimer went on dreamily. "A coat and waistcoat from Weston! I do wish I had seen them. His cut is said to be exquisite, you know, and he scarcely uses any padding. Even Harry must have looked quite presentable."

"I expect Mr. Drew's coats *all* come from Mr. Weston," said Miss Spencer grimly. "You will have every opportunity, Letty, to study expensive London tailoring at first hand."

Letty pricked up her ears. "Mr. Drew? Who, pray, is Mr. Drew?" She looked around the room, as though the unknown gentleman might be hiding somewhere. Then, to her utter astonishment, Miss Spencer reacted to this innocent enquiry by putting her face in her hands and bursting into tears—a happening so unprecedented and so unlike her that Miss Lorrimer could only gape at her friend in silent dismay, until she recovered enough of her senses to hasten to Katherine's side to offer comfort. After a few moments, Katherine rallied and, in a tolerably steady voice, was able to tell Letty of the dreadful news concerning Mr. Drew and Kielder.

Miss Lorrimer was obliged to sit down suddenly. "Kate! It cannot be true! Such things do not happen!"

"They can and they have."

"Poor, poor Kate! No wonder you are so upset. I know how much Kielder means to you. And that Will should lose his inheritance . . . oh, it is too *horrible* to contemplate! That odious, *odious* brother of yours! I know one should not speak ill of the dead, but if Harry were here I declare I should murder him! It is too bad! Where will you go? What will you do?"

Miss Spencer blew her nose. "We may stay here for the present—by Mr. Drew's leave. He is not proposing to turn us out of our home immediately. He is all generosity! I have asked him if he will sell Kielder back to us."

"Sell you back your own home!" Letty shook her spiky head at the unfairness of it all. "What did he say?"

"He will not give me an answer directly. He said—" Katherine screwed up her handkerchief in her fist. "He said he will be more likely to consider selling it back if I . . . if I make myself agreeable to him."

Miss Lorrimer's mouth fell open. "Make yourself agreeable to him? What could he mean? You do not think . . . ? Could he have intended—"

"No, of course not! Don't be absurd, Letty. You have been reading too many novels. It's just that Harry presented me in a very disagreeable light, it seems. Mr. Drew imagines me to be some kind of virago."

"How unjust! It was Harry who behaved so abominably! You tried so hard. If Mr. Drew thinks—"

"I am not in the least concerned with what Mr. Drew thinks of me, Letty. I really do not care. And I am not going to be in the least agreeable to him. He is the most insufferable, conceited creature—all London finery and fancy manners. You should see him bow. How I *dislike* him!"

"How does he bow?" asked Miss Lorrimer with interest.

"*Very* low. Like this." Miss Spencer gave a passable imitation.

"Is he—is he a *dandy*?" Letty breathed.

"I really could not say," Katherine said impatiently. "You could judge for yourself, but he has not risen yet. I daresay the *ton* do not bestir themselves much before midday."

Miss Lorrimer tried hard to look disappointed.

"To be sure, I believe they do not. A dandy takes a great deal of time to dress, you know. Everything must be perfect in their attire. They must tie their neck handkerchiefs in the latest style, and *that* is quite an art; the hair must be combed just so, the footwear highly polished and without a speck of dust."

"Really?" said Miss Spencer sardonically. "I suppose that is all they have to do all day so it does not matter how long it takes."

"Oh, no. Once they are dressed they are ready to enjoy all the diversions that London can offer," Miss Lorrimer explained. "Concerts, theatres, assemblies, balls, ridottos, drums . . ."

"Unfortunately for him, Mr. Drew will find that once he is dressed and ready there is nowhere to go. Northumberland has very few of those things to offer."

"That is true," Letty said mournfully. "How humiliating for us! And how dull for Mr. Drew!"

"What does it matter how dull it is for him? The duller the better. I hope you are not feeling sorry for him, Letty!"

"Of course not! It's—it's just that I should not like us to be thought complete provincials."

"I do not care if he thinks us the dreariest provincials he has ever met! You are not to be nice to him when you meet him, Letty, or I shall have you shown out."

"Indeed, I shall not be, Kate. I promise," Miss Lorrimer protested. Then she added, with a little rush, "But you will not object if I ask him one or two small questions as to the latest fashions?"

"There would be no point in my objecting," Katherine said with a smile, "because I know you could not prevent yourself. Ask him all you wish."

"Thank you, dear Kate! But I shall not smile at him, I vow. I shall look very cold and severe—like this."

Letty tried to compose her pretty features into coldness and severity, but it was so much against nature that she merely looked ridiculous, and they both began to laugh. Katherine suddenly became serious again. She went to the window and stood looking out onto the moors that stretched away below the castle as far as the distant Cheviot Hills. The rugged expanse of grass, heather, and peat looked much as it had done since the beginning of history. It was the haunt of grouse and curlews, lapwings and sheep; the home of everything that was wild and beautiful. Mr. Drew and his kind had no place here, no right to it at all. She leaned her forehead against the glass.

"I do not know what I shall do if Mr. Drew refuses to sell Kielder back, Letty. I could not bear to lose it."

"Perhaps he may not like it, Kate," Miss Lorrimer said cheeringly. "After all, you must admit, although I daresay you will not, that it is a very draughty, uncomfortable sort of place to live. It is all very well for you—you are accustomed to it. But Mr. Drew may decide that he does not care for it after all."

Miss Spencer did not answer for a moment. Then she turned suddenly from the window, her dark eyes alight with excitement.

"Why, Letty, you have just shown me what I must do!"

"Have I?"

"Yes. It is so simple I do not know why I did not think of it before."

"Think of *what*, Kate? Do tell me!"

"Well . . . I do agree that Kielder is a little damp and draughty."

"You do?" Letty said, amazed. It was something that Katherine usually denied vigourously.

"Yes. It is quite true. But not enough. We must make it far, far worse."

"Must we?" queried Letty, doubtfully.

Miss Spencer began to pace about the room. "Of course. Don't you see, Letty? We must make it so bad that Mr. Drew cannot support to live here. It should not be so difficult: I am sure he has been used to every comfort. Let me see . . . To begin with, we could break some more windows to make the draughts worse. Then we could contrive some new holes in the roof so that the rain leaks in even more. And we could block up the chimney in the great hall, so that it smokes very badly . . ."

"Are you sure that is a good idea, Kate?"

"It is an *excellent* idea. And you will help me, won't you, Letty. Will is too young to be much use, and Nurse is too old. I cannot ask poor old Purves—he would be shocked. Say you will help me!"

Miss Lorrimer jumped to her feet and hugged her friend. "Of course I shall, Kate."

"And you will come and stay—just for a few days?"

Letty nobly thrust to one side all thought of the snug warmth of Langley Grange and suppressed, too, any image of Kielder worse than it was already. "Willingly, Kate. I shall come at once. Today."

"Will your papa allow it?"

"If it is to help *you*, he will certainly do so. You know how much he admires you."

"Thank you, Letty."

"And I have another idea for you."

"Is it a good one?"

"The best! One of us could dress up as a ghost and frighten Mr. Drew out of his wits! We could pretend to be one of your old ancestresses. Have you one that was beheaded? That would do capitally!"

"Letty, that *is* the best idea! How clever of you! Mr. Drew will soon learn that Kielder is not at all to his taste. Perhaps he will then go back to his two homes in the South."

"Did you say *two* homes, Kate? He must be rich."

"I suppose he must be," said Miss Spencer, uninterested.

"How old is he?"

"I could not say precisely. A year or two older than me, perhaps."

"Is he—is he handsome?"

"Very," Katherine said shortly.

"Oh dear," sighed Miss Lorrimer. "Young, rich and handsome . . . It is going to be very difficult for me to dislike him as I should."

At that moment Purves appeared in the doorway to announce that Mr. Webber had called to see Miss Spencer.

"Vernon!" said Katherine, without much enthusiasm. "I shall have to see him, or he will be offended. Show him up, please, Purves."

"Is he in love with you or me just now?" Letty enquired when the butler had withdrawn. "It is as well to know, then one can be prepared."

"It must be me, since he is calling here. How tiresome! I expect he is going to propose again."

"Perhaps one of us should give in and marry him," Letty suggested gravely. "Then we should all have some peace. Sudley Hall is very pleasant, you know, Kate. The east wing is not all that it might be, to be sure, but it could always be pulled down."

"Vernon's mama is not all that she might be either," Katherine rejoined. "And *she* could not be pulled down. I know you are only joking, Letty, but you are never to consider such a thought. He would bore you to tears within the week. As for me, I should make him miserable and he would drive me mad."

"Then we shall both die old maids," Letty said mournfully. "Who else but Vernon is ever going to offer for us?"

A heavy tread could be heard approaching. Katherine

put her finger to her lips. "I shall have to tell him about Mr. Drew, Letty—he will learn it soon enough. But do not say a word about our plan—you know how very proper he is. And put your bonnet on, before he sees your hair. He will not understand about it being all the crack, and you will get a dreadful scolding."

Miss Lorrimer quickly obeyed, and when the very proper gentleman entered the room he found the two ladies, both of whom he had known since childhood, awaiting him demurely. Being also the perfect gentleman, he concealed his chagrin at finding Miss Lorrimer present. At their last meeting at Langley Grange, he had reached the regrettable decision that she would not, after all, make a suitable mistress for Sudley Hall. He had discovered a frivolous element in her makeup, which did not augur well: the joke she had played on him when she had hidden his hat had not been the kind of behaviour he looked for in a wife. There was also the unfortunate Connexion with Trade. He himself would have been prepared to overlook this, since the connexion was such a profitable one—after all, Sudley Hall was expensive to keep up—but his mama was not so liberal in her views and had withheld her blessing. After due consideration, he had returned to his original opinion that Katherine, although possessed of no fortune and not so pretty, was nonetheless of faultless breeding and of a sober behaviour properly befitting the station to which she would be called. He therefore bowed longest and lowest to Miss Spencer, who, observing the clumsy and labourious operation this involved, could not help calling to mind the effortless elegance of Mr. Drew.

Mr. Webber was in his late twenties, but seemed considerably older. He was medium in height, medium in build, medium in colouring and complexion; in fact, he was medium in most respects, save for a decided *embonpoint* which could already be detected beneath his plain buff-coloured waistcoat. It was not hard to imagine how he would look in ten years time.

"Good morning, Katherine. Good morning, Letitia."
A very cursory glance towards Letty. "I trust I find you
in good health."

Civilities having been exchanged on all sides, it became quickly apparent to the ladies that it was indeed
Miss Spencer who was the favoured one. Mr. Webber
addressed himself chiefly to her, with a ponderous determination, and Katherine, conscious of Letty's stifled
giggles, was hard put to it to keep a serious face. In
desperation, she cut short a long monologue on the
attractions of Sudley Hall compared with Kielder by
informing him of her news. He was as shocked as Letty
had been and walked about the room, hands behind his
back, saying that it was outrageous, disgraceful, infamous . . . and that he had always known that Harry was
a wastrel—if Katherine would forgive him for saying so.
After some more proclamations on the subject and assur-
ances that something would be done about it, it came
suddenly into his thoughts that the event might work to
his advantage, since Katherine's lack of a home might
render her more willing and ready to accept the alternative of Sudley Hall, which she had hitherto persisted in
refusing. With this in view, he surprised his audience by
falling quite silent. The additional information from
Miss Lorrimer, however, that Mr. Drew was actually at
the castle now, prompted him to issue an immediate
invitation to Katherine to remove to Sudley forthwith.

"For you cannot stay here. You must see that. It would
not do at all. Not at all! Mama would be delighted to
receive you."

"How thoughtful of you, Vernon—though I rather
doubt your mother's delight—but I have no intention of
leaving yet, I promise you. Mr. Drew is allowing us to
stay for a while, and so long as there is any hope of
regaining Kielder, I propose to remain."

"What hope could there be?"

"He may decide to sell it back to us. He may come to
realise"—Katherine caught Letty's eye and looked

quickly away—"that it does not . . . suit. So, for the present, I shall stay."

"And so shall I," Letty added. "I am coming to visit at Kielder, so you need not worry, Vernon."

But Mr. Webber looked even more worried. It all sounded highly undesirable, not to say improper, to him, and the circumstances were not at all those he would have wished for his intended. He was quite certain that Mama would not approve. Furthermore, the presence of Letitia at the castle, let alone that of Mr. Drew himself, would scarcely be conducive to his plan of courtship. It was expedient to remove Katherine from Kielder, but he could not see exactly how he could achieve this, other than by force. There was a stubbornness about her that he had encountered more than once before—especially concerning anything to do with her family and home.

He was about to argue the point further, in the hope of making Katherine see reason, when the door was flung wide and Will came dashing into the room, followed closely by a panting Boots. Mr. Webber looked with disapproval at his beloved's small brother; he considered Will to be unruly and lacking in the proper respect due to his elders, but he had more sense than to say so. To criticise any member of the Spencer family had always been to invite Katherine's fierce defence; he had never even dared speak ill of Harry at his very worst. Privately, it was Vernon's opinion that unless some discipline was instilled into the boy soon, the fourteenth baronet would go the way of the thirteenth.

Seeing his sister's frown, Will remembered his manners and gave Miss Lorrimer and Mr. Webber a hasty, if belated bow. He then held up a large and rusty key, which he dangled before them triumphantly.

"I've done it!" he announced with a beaming smile, and the spaniel barked, as if to underline his share in the achievement.

"Done *what*, Will?" Katherine asked, exasperated. "You really must not rush into rooms like that."

"I've locked him in the dungeon!"

"What! What are you talking about?"

"Mr. *Drew*. I've locked him in the dungeon!"

Letty gave a small shriek. The smile on Will's face faded as he looked at the varied expressions of the three people before him: Miss Lorrimer's shuddering horror, Mr. Webber's scandalised disapproval, and the mixture of dismay, disapprobation, and then a strange thoughtfulness passing over his sister's face in rapid succession. Boots, sensing unexpected trouble, drooped his ears and tail guiltily.

Miss Spencer found her voice first. "You had better explain yourself, Will. Just what exactly have you done?"

Her brother looked sulky and kicked at the carpet with the toe of his shoe. "Mr. Drew asked me to show him round the castle. He wanted to see it all. While we were going up the north tower I had this wonderful idea. . . . He was bound to want to see the dungeon—everybody does. I thought if I could manage to lock him in, then we could keep him there until he had promised to tear up Harry's voucher and give us back Kielder. We could feed him through the grill—just like they did prisoners in the old days. It was easy. He went inside to see it better and I just slammed the door shut on him and locked it." He looked at Katherine reproachfully. "I thought you would be pleased. I did it for you. I thought you wanted Kielder back."

Mr. Webber could contain his outrage no longer. "What you have done is disgraceful, William! Have you no shame? Have you no sense of decency? To lock someone—*anyone*—in a dungeon is the height of ill manners!"

"Are there rats?" asked Letty faintly.

"Bound to be," said Will, with scornful relish. "There are rats and mice everywhere in the castle."

Miss Lorrimer uttered a moan and clutched at a chair to support herself. Mr. Webber stepped forward, assuming authority.

"We must release Mr. Drew at once. Hand me that key, William."

"One moment, Vernon," Katherine intervened. "You are forgetting, I think, that this is our concern: it is our key, our dungeon, and *our* prisoner."

He stared at her uncomprehending. "You are surely not proposing to keep him there one minute longer. . . ." Seeing her expression, he went on, less certainly. "You must see, Katherine, that William has behaved abominably—the whole idea is preposterous!"

"I have been thinking," she said consideringly. "It might not do any harm to leave him there—for a few hours at least. Then he might quickly reach the conclusion that Kielder would not suit him after all."

"Kate, you really should not," Letty clasped her hands anxiously. "Think of the *rats*!"

"I *am* thinking of them," she answered in a vehement whisper. "Don't you see, Letty? It is just what is needed to give him a good fright!"

"It is unthinkable!" Mr. Webber expostulated, unable to credit his ears. "And unbecoming in you, Katherine—if I may say so—to consider such a thing for even a moment."

"No, you may not say so, Vernon. Any more than you may censure Will. That is *my* affair. He acted with the best of intentions—that of saving Kielder—and I do not think he should be blamed for it."

"Really, Katherine. I find myself at a loss for words—"

"I am very thankful to hear it, Vernon. Letty, what shall we do? Shall we leave Mr. Drew to his fate?"

Miss Lorrimer had recovered her equilibrium and, with it, a little common sense. "I think we should not, Kate. Only consider that to do so might have the very *reverse* effect. Mr. Drew might be so incensed by such treatment that he might refuse ever to consider selling Kielder back to you. And," she added meaningfully, "there are *other ways* . . . remember."

"I suppose you may be right," Katherine said regretfully. "We had better go down and let him out. What a waste and what a pity!"

The dungeon at Kielder was reached by a flight of steep and slippery steps which descended into the bowels of the earth beneath the castle. Candle held high, Will led the way. Miss Spencer followed, then Mr. Webber, who had been determined not to be left behind, and finally Miss Lorrimer, who would willingly have stayed behind had she not been insatiably curious about the prisoner. The air below ground was cold and dank. Water trickled horribly down the walls, and the darkness beyond the candle's reach was impenetrably black. Every smallest sound echoed and re-echoed about them, and Letty, who imagined the place to be infested with monstrous, yellow-fanged rodents, gave little shrieks and cries at every step. At length, Will halted the party before a great oak door, stoutly banded with iron, a grill set in the centre and two bolts top and bottom with a lock between.

Mr. Webber bustled forward. He slid the shutter of the grill to one side and called through it in dramatic tones, "Mr. Drew! Mr. Drew! We have come to release you! Help is at hand!"

There was no response from beyond the door. Nothing could be heard but the drip of water from the roof nearby and a small scratching sound closer at hand which caused Letty to squeal again.

"Be quiet, Letitia!" Mr. Webber admonished her. "This is very grave. I am much afraid that Mr. Drew may have been taken ill . . . or worse. Give me the key at once."

Will handed it over reluctantly. Key and bolts grated loudly in the silence. Mr. Webber turned the handle and it swung open inwards, revealing the top of another flight of stone steps, which led down into the depths of the dungeon itself. Silence. Miss Spencer and Miss Lorrimer exchanged rather anxious glances, and Will looked suddenly terrified.

"Give me the candle, Will," Katherine said at last. "I shall go down."

Nobody demurred or volunteered to take her place. She took the light and began to make her way cautiously down the steps. Green slime glistened on the walls and on the flagged floor below. She shuddered. It was a long while since she had visited this dreadful place, and with good reason: in this chill and terrible black hole prisoners had been incarcerated for months, even years on end, without light or fresh air or any contact with the outside world except their jailer. Men had died here, diseased, demented, and forgotten. It was one part of the Spencer history of which she could not be proud. The thought of anyone—even Mr. Drew—spending more than five minutes shut up in here was now so appalling that she was ashamed of ever having thought of it. Katherine inched her way down two more steps and swept the candle from left to right. The dungeon appeared to be empty, and yet this was impossible. He could not have escaped. There was no way out, as other men had found to their despair centuries ago. Her heart pounding with dread, she hurried to the bottom of the steps and searched before her again. . . . There was nobody there.

Suddenly, she was seized from behind in a grip so fierce and strong that she could not move: a hand was clamped over her mouth, stifling her scream, and an arm encircled her neck so tightly that she could hardly breathe.

"Good morning, Miss Spencer," Mr. Drew said silkily in her right ear. His breath was warm against her cheek. "Is this how you usually treat your visitors to Kielder? Is it a northern custom, perhaps?"

She shook her head and tried to speak but could not. He took his hand away from her mouth but still held her close against him with his arm around her neck.

42

"I'm sorry," she croaked. "Will meant no harm."

"Didn't he?" he said in a voice quite unlike the drink-slurred one of the evening before. "Do you expect me to believe that? And I'm not sure I should blame him if he did. What a convenient way to rid the Spencers of an unfortunate threat to the family. An alternative to the boiling oil over the ramparts."

"I assure you, we were not going to leave you here—"

"I think *you* would have done. I know you are capable of anything where Kielder is concerned, Miss Spencer."

She could not see his face to know whether he was in earnest or not, but sensed that he was smiling as he spoke. There was a sound above them, and Mr. Webber's tones echoed round the chamber.

"Katherine! Mr. Drew! Are you there?"

"Where else could we be?" she said impatiently.

Drew laughed then. "Who is that numbskull who keeps calling me?"

"Mr. Webber. If you would let me go you could see for yourself."

"I am not perfectly sure that I want to do either," he said, sounding amused. But he released her nonetheless. "Lead on, then."

Katherine rubbed her neck ruefully; he was stronger than she would have believed possible, and she felt bruised and shaken. She lighted their way up the steps, and as they emerged from the doorway, Mr. Webber was full of agonised apologies for something for which he was in no way to blame.

"My dear sir . . . what can I say? Such an unfortunate occurrence . . . a most *unhappy* happening! I cannot begin to tell you how sorry I am. . . ."

Mr. Drew dismissed these lamentations.

"If you cannot begin, please do not trouble yourself further," he said pleasantly.

He turned with a bow and a smile to Miss Lorrimer, who, to Miss Spencer's disgust, sank into a quite unnecessarily deep curtsey, heedless of either the dirt or the rats. Even in the dim and flickering candlelight, Letty had noted instantly the quilted waistcoat with its double row of small buttons; the starched points of the white collar revealing two cravats, a black satin one over a white one. She had recognised unerringly and with absolute enchantment that here before her, at long last, was the very epitome of the dandy.

== 3 ==

MISS LORRIMER, AS good as her word, sent to Langley Grange for her clothes and prepared to stay at Kielder for as long as she was needed. That she did so with considerably more eagerness than previously did not pass unnoticed by Miss Spencer, who commented somewhat acidly on Letty's unnecessarily deferential attitude to Mr. Drew.

"There is not the slightest need to curtsey quite so low whenever he appears, Letty. He is not royalty, you know."

"But he has such style and elegance, Kate, that he might almost be."

"He is plain Mr. Drew—that is all. I do not understand how you can find him so impressive. He is the vainest person I have ever met. He may be handsome, I grant you, but he knows it too well."

"I do not think he could be called vain, Kate. He never once looks at himself in the glass, as Harry was always doing. Even Vernon is forever stealing glances at himself when he thinks nobody is watching, though what pleasure that can give him, I really cannot imagine. If I were him I should *never* look in the glass at all."

Katherine smiled. "Well, at least there is one good thing that has come of all this. Vernon disapproves of us both so strongly now that neither of us is presently in any danger of being proposed to for some time."

"He is overawed by Mr. Drew. Did you notice? He bowed at least ten times before he left."

"No more times than you curtsied, I daresay," Katherine said pointedly. "You are both as bad as each other, Letty, and no support to me at all."

"I shall try very hard from now on," Miss Lorrimer promised. "But, Kate, he is so agreeable! It is very difficult. If I were him I should have been exceedingly angry at being shut up in that dreadful dungeon. He seemed almost amused, and quite forgave Will. It is fortunate that he is still well disposed towards you."

"I really do not care whether he is or not, Letty. I have no intention of abandoning our plan just because Mr. Drew is *agreeable*. I propose to make Kielder as uncomfortable for him as possible and I shall start by blocking up the great hall chimney so that the fire smokes this evening. We can also break a windowpane or two. That should make it quite cold."

Miss Lorrimer shivered. "It seems cold enough already to me. I'm sure he will be uncomfortable as things are."

"No. It must be made much worse."

This was beyond Letty's imagining, but she loyally did not say so. Another thought had just occurred to her. "Have you considered, Kate, that Mr. Drew might very well sell Kielder to someone else? He does not have to sell it to you."

Miss Spencer went very still. "I had not thought of that. But surely not even he would stoop so low. At any rate, it is a risk we shall have to take."

She looked so despondent for a moment that Letty felt the need to give some encouragement.

"Don't forget the ghost, Kate. That should be fun! Whom shall we invent for your headless ancestress?"

"There is no need to invent anyone. We already have a perfectly adequate ghost. Lady Harriet."

"L-lady Harriet?"

"Yes. Have I never told you about her? She was the

first wife of the eighth baronet. Poor thing, it is a very sad story. She had such an unhappy life. Her husband was a brute and ill-treated her disgracefully. He had a string of mistresses and used to parade them in front of her."

"How shocking!" said Letty indignantly.

"Yes, wasn't it? Her only child—a son—died when he was two years old. She went mad with grief and was locked up in the north tower, where she died ten years later. It is said that she walks the castle at night, looking for her lost son."

"D-does she? Have you ever seen her, Kate?"

"No. But I have felt her presence at times . . . known for certain that she was there, somewhere in the castle. One of the footmen saw her once quite clearly on the north tower stairs."

"How did he know it was Lady Harriet?" Letty asked, rather pale.

"There is a portrait of her in the long gallery. She is wearing a blue gown, very magnificent, with a lace ruff and many jewels. The footman recognised her."

Letty was liking less and less the idea of wandering about the castle at night, impersonating any ghost. "If Lady Harriet is likely to appear herself," she said hopefully, "then there is really no need for us to do anything. We may leave it all in her hands."

Miss Spencer shook her head. "We cannot rely on her, Letty. Or on her being seen by Mr. Drew. We shall have to dress up ourselves." Seeing the pale face before her she added reassuringly, "Don't worry. I shall play the part. You need only help me with the costume."

"Have you told Will any of this?"

"No, and I shall say nothing to him for the present. He is incapable of keeping a secret. Besides, he has decided that Mr. Drew is a famous fellow, since he forgave him so readily, and since he promised to take him out shooting."

"Harry always refused to take him, didn't he? I wonder if Mr. Drew is a good marksman."

"Of course he is not! How could a dandy know how to shoot properly," Katherine said scornfully. "I doubt he even knows how to hold a gun. In any case, Boots will see that he does not hit anything."

"*Boots?* What has he to do with it?"

"I offered him to Mr. Drew as a gun dog today. I told him that he was an excellent retriever."

"But Kate, Boots has never retrieved in his life! He is untrainable! If you tell him to do one thing, he does quite another!"

"Exactly." Katherine smiled wickedly. "And Boots will be running about on the moors now, scattering grouse to the four winds. It will take the finest marksman in Northumberland to hit anything!"

"Kate, you are incorrigible! What will Mr. Drew say? He will not forgive this so readily."

"I daresay he will not even know how a gun dog should behave. And while he is safely absent, Letty, we can block up the chimney!"

An apprehensive Miss Lorrimer assisted in collecting together a bundle of old sheets from the linen cupboard, in dampening them thoroughly, and in bearing them, heavy and dripping, to the big fireplace. It proved far more difficult than they had anticipated to lodge the bundle firmly and high enough in the wide chimney. Soot showered down upon them as they poked and prodded the sheeting into place with the aid of broom handles. But for the good fortune of there being a ledge on each side part of the way up, the task would have been impossible. When it was finally finished they both looked like sweeps themselves, with black hands and faces, and red-rimmed eyes. Letty gamely disregarded the damage done to her gown.

"Do you think it will serve, Kate?"

"I trust so. We shall see this evening. But do not forget on any account, Letty, that you must not appear at all surprised. Remember, the chimney always smokes."

But when Miss Spencer descended the stairs to the great hall several hours later, there was not a wisp of smoke to be seen. Purves, bent on one arthritic knee, was trying to coax life into the wood with the bellows.

"I cannot understand it, ma'am," he said worriedly. "We never have any trouble with this fire usually. The one in the library can be difficult if the wind is in the north, but this one—it always catches at once."

He struggled on for a few moments with the huge bellows; the fire responded briefly before relapsing again.

"Perhaps the wood is too damp, Purves," Katherine suggested, anxious to spare the old man further effort. "Let us wait awhile and see if it catches."

The butler rose creakily to his feet. "Very well, ma'am."

He went away, puzzled and reluctant and shaking his grey head. As he did so, Will came tearing into the hall, his face glowing and triumphant. He was followed by a wet and muddy Boots, who flung himself down in an exhausted heap before the feeble glow.

"I have had such a capital time, Kate!" Will told her eagerly. "You cannot imagine what fun it has been out on the moors. I shot a grouse, you know! My very first!"

"Well done," said Miss Spencer rather reservedly.

"Mr. Drew bagged thirty or more," her brother went on enthusiastically. "He is an excellent shot. Even Fowler was impressed, and you know how hard he is to please! Every bird killed outright—no winging 'em, like Harry used to do."

If Mr. Drew had won the approval of the head game-keeper, who was a dour old Scot, then he must indeed be a good shot. This was not at all what Katherine wished to hear; she quite expected the contrary—that he had missed every bird and made a complete fool of himself. Boots must have failed her utterly.

"And you should have seen Boots," Will went on happily. "I never thought he'd be any good. Couldn't understand why Mr. Drew took him at all. I told him he was the worst trained dog in the world and would make a dreadful nuisance of himself, but he took no notice. He seemed to think it was rather a joke! Anyway, Boots did every single thing he told him! Just as he should! Mr. Drew has a way with animals, Kate, I could tell—"

"You are quite forgetting who Mr. Drew is, Will. I do not wish to hear you singing his praises."

Will sat down on the stool near the fireside; there was a streak of mud across his pink cheek. "Oh, I know all that, Kate. But it is not his fault, is it? He cannot help what Harry did." He looked up defiantly. "I like him a lot better than Harry, too. *He* never took me out shooting."

"You are being absurd, Will. Just because Mr. Drew takes you out on what should by rights have been your own moors to shoot at your own game, there is no need to be so—so *grateful* for it!"

The baronet shrugged his shoulders and picked up the poker to prod at the smouldering logs beside him. "I say, Kate, whatever's the matter with the fire? It's not burning at all."

"Will, you must listen to me," she persisted. "I do not wish you to be friendly with Mr. Drew. It is a matter of pride, and of family honour. Don't you see—"

But he was not listening. He was busily poking at the fire, making little showers of sparks as he moved the logs about; a narrow tongue of flame leapt high, and as it did so, a puff of smoke blew back from the hearth. He coughed. "There! That's better. It was laid all wrong." He put down the poker and, looking up, smiled suddenly. "Oh, good evening, Mr. Drew."

Miss Spencer turned. Mr. Drew was watching them from the staircase, and she wondered how much he had overheard of their conversation. For a moment she understood something of Letty's admiration for sartorial elegance: his blue coat, quilted waistcoat, black pantaloons, and black, varnished shoes were clearly of the very first style of fashion and worn with a superb nonchalance. His cravat looked exquisitely tied in the most complicated way, which she knew Harry could never have hoped to emulate. It was impossible to imagine that he had been anywhere near the moors or involved himself in anything so muddy and uncomfortable as shooting game. It was also impossible to deny that he presented an extraordinarily handsome appearance, but this thought was easily and quickly suppressed by reminding herself—just as she had reminded her small brother—of who this man was. Not only had he taken Kielder from them, but he was a drunkard, like Harry—a gambler and a rake.

He came towards them.

"I was telling Kate about the shoot," Will said.

He looked at her with a smile. "I was agreeably surprised, Miss Spencer. I recollect that you thought the shooting poor. It was quite the contrary. And I am indebted to you for providing me with such a magnificent gun dog. The credit must go to Boots for the day's bag. He is superb!"

Will gave a snort of laughter. "Did Kate tell you to take Boots? I wondered why. He has always been useless until now."

The subject of the conversation looked up at mention of his name, wagged his tail tiredly and fell back asleep once more.

"He must come out with me again," Mr. Drew said solemnly. "He brings me good fortune."

"Will you take me as well?" Will asked eagerly.

"If your sister permits."

"I should not wish William to make a nuisance of himself. I think it preferable he does not."

"I enjoy his company," he said. "I have no brother, only a sister who is six years younger than I, and a poor companion by comparison."

A wreath of blue smoke now hung above the hearth. Miss Spencer coughed and moved a little away. Will had picked up the poker again and was jabbing wildly at the logs. More sparks flew up and thick smoke belched forth. Miss Lorrimer, descending the staircase at that moment, observed the scene with satisfaction.

"Good gracious, the chimney is smoking again!" she cried. "I really do not know how you support living here, Kate. If it isn't one thing, it is another! The draughts are dreadful and everything is damp. I'm sure *I* could not endure it for more than a month." She choked a little at the smoke. "You must find the North very uncivilised, Mr. Drew. I am persuaded you do not suffer such inconveniences in your home in the South."

"Oh, we have smoking chimneys and draughts in plenty," he replied. "I am quite accustomed to them. All old places are the same."

"I cannot believe that anything could be as bad as Kielder," Letty declared, and then wondered, as she saw the frown on Katherine's face, if she had gone too far.

"The chimney has never smoked before," Will said, staring at the fire.

"Nonsense," his sister said at once. "It is always doing so. There is nothing to be done about it."

The smoke was now so bad that they were obliged to retreat—all except Mr. Drew, who moved to the fire and kicked aside the smouldering logs with the toe of his shoe. The smoke abated.

"There is something obstructing the chimney," he said calmly. "It can soon be dealt with."

"I have told you that this chimney always smokes," Katherine insisted.

"And I do not believe you, Miss Spencer."

Purves was despatched to fetch a long pole. As they waited, Letty glanced apprehensively at Miss Spencer, but her friend had turned away. The butler, returning with a pole, lowered himself painfully onto one knee to investigate.

"There is certainly an obstruction there, sir," he said. "I can feel it."

Mr. Drew said nothing, but he looked at Miss Spencer. The butler continued to prod with the pole, until at last pieces of scorched linen began to fall down into the hearth. A final thrust, and the whole blackened bundle tumbled into the grate. There was silence whilst they all stared at it. Letty giggled nervously.

"Good heavens! How ever did that get up there?"

"I thought perhaps Miss Spencer might have some idea," Mr. Drew said.

She turned to face him. "None whatever," she said unblushingly.

He smiled. "Not even the smallest notion, Miss Spencer?"

"Not even the smallest, Mr. Drew."

At dinner no further mention was made of the odd circumstance of the blocked chimney. Mr. Drew conversed amiably, Letty feverishly, and Will eagerly, whenever the discussion touched upon the day's shooting. Miss Spencer, however, remained for the most part silent.

"Do tell me please, Mr. Drew," Miss Lorrimer requested during one of these long silences, "whether the ladies are wearing their hair like this in London—*à la* Titus? Is mine just the way it should be?"

He considered her gravely for a moment. "No, Miss Lorrimer, it is not at all as it should be. In the first place, the cut is wrong, and in the second, the fashion is outdated."

Letty looked crestfallen, but rallied quickly. "Oh, well. I daresay it will grow out soon enough. And what of my gown, Mr. Drew? It is copied faithfully from *The Lady's Magazine.*"

"Since you ask my opinion, I will tell you that your gown, charming as it may be, is at least five years out of fashion, if not more. It is far too long. It should reach the ankles only. Also, the skirts are too full, and standing collars are no longer worn." He raised his eyeglass and scrutinised her carefully. "I should aim for simplicity, Miss Lorrimer, if I were you. Do away with all those ribbons and frills; it would become you vastly better."

Letty, far from resenting the criticism, was delighted with the advice. "I shall remember what you say, Mr. Drew. Indeed I shall! Thank you. There, Kate—I told you that we are the veriest country bumpkins where fashion is concerned. It is quite tragic!"

Mr. Drew drank some wine. "I do not think that Miss Spencer shares your interest in fashion, Miss Lorrimer."

"No, I do not," Katherine said, putting down her knife with a clatter. "I do not give a fig for fashion. I do not care a jot what a person may be wearing—whether it is five, ten, or twenty years out of date. I do not consider it is important. Fine clothes do not make fine people, Mr. Drew."

"I don't deny it," he said, smiling across the table at her.

"I imagine, though, that clothes must constitute one of your chief interests in life."

"No, I have others."

"Such as gambling?"

"Such as gambling," he agreed. "Hunting is another. In agreeable company, of course, and so long as one does not trouble oneself to go beyond the first few fields."

Miss Spencer stared. "Is that what you call hunting, Mr. Drew? To go no further than a few fields?"

"Certainly," he said lazily. "Otherwise one would run the risk of becoming intolerably splashed and muddy, you see. And what would be the point of that?" He drank some more wine. "I leave all that sort of thing to the rustics."

If any further proof were needed of the rightness of her opinion of Mr. Drew's character, this was it. To abandon the hunt after a field or two rather than get oneself muddy was beneath contempt. Despite the failure of the blocked chimney, Katherine's hopes were suddenly raised: any man who could abandon a hunt in order to save himself discomfort might also abandon a cold and draughty castle for the same reason.

After dinner they returned to the great hall, where the fire was now blazing away merrily. Katherine fetched the chessboard and pieces from the armoire and, as was her nightly habit, sat down to play a game with her brother. Letty picked up her embroidery—a somewhat mangled affair which she struggled with each evening—while Mr. Drew stood near the chess table, watching for a while, his arms folded across his chest. Will looked up.

"Kate always wins," he said ruefully.

"Your sister is a good tactician in many ways," Mr. Drew acknowledged. "But she sometimes makes the mistake of allowing her opponent to anticipate her next move."

"Well, *I* never know what it is," the boy said despairingly as his knight was captured and removed from the board.

"If I were you I should play my queen knight to the second square of the king file."

"Would you, sir?" Will looked doubtful. "But . . . oh, well, if you're sure."

He did so with blind faith, and his sister, with the

contrary opinion of this advice, promptly took her brother's king pawn, which had been left unprotected by the move.

"What now, sir?" Will asked with some bitterness.

The loss of the pawn had not appeared to worry Mr. Drew.

"Advance your queen bishop pawn one square."

With a small shrug Will complied, hunching his shoulders dispiritedly. Miss Spencer bit her lip and frowned at the board. Her unguarded capture of the pawn had given her the considerable pleasure of proving Mr. Drew's unsolicited counsel to be wrong, but now she saw, too late, that this second move threatened her advanced bishop. She had no choice but to move the bishop away to safety—a retreat which destroyed carefully laid plans which could have brought her victory within three moves.

Will glanced enquiringly up at his mentor.

"Your queen," was the laconic reply.

The boy looked again at the board and saw suddenly that he could now play his queen all the way along a diagonal opened by the removal of the white bishop. And, not only that, in advancing his queen he threatened his sister's knight. He beamed with pleasure.

Miss Spencer, however, did not smile. She saw that she had foolishly fallen into a trap. She could not move her king out of check and at the same time protect her knight. She must lose the piece and, with it, any prospect of imminent victory. Worse, there was even the unthinkable possibility of defeat. The game had now resolved itself into a contest between herself and Mr. Drew, and she had made the fatal mistake of underestimating him. A dandy could, it seemed, play chess, and play it well. Rather pettishly Katherine put her king out of check and, as she had anticipated, had to watch the immediate despatch of her knight. Her next move was a flustered and desperate attempt to retrieve the situation by bringing her bishop back into the fray.

"Queen knight," Mr. Drew murmured laconically.

Dismayed, Katherine realised that she had moved her bishop to within the black knight's reach, and her brother swooped upon the piece with gusto. Letty, intrigued, put down her needlework, which was boring her exceedingly, and came to stand beside Mr. Drew. Miss Spencer, nettled and unnerved, advanced her king knight pawn one rank.

Will raised his head.

"Your queen knight again," Mr. Drew told him quietly. "Use him right and the game is yours, Sir William."

Will stared hard at the board and then with a wild whoop of joy picked up the black knight and moved him to the sixth square of the queen file.

"Checkmate!"

Miss Spencer saw that this was indisputably the case: to move her king out of the reach of Will's knight would only bring him into the range of the black queen. In short, she could do nothing but concede defeat. The game was Will's—or rather, Mr. Drew's, and matters were not improved by Letty clapping loudly, nor by Will crowing like a young cockerel.

"I've won! I've won!" he shouted, jumping up and dancing about, whilst Boots, awoken from a deep and peaceful slumber, staggered to his feet and lolloped about after the excited boy, anxious not to be excluded from the fun.

"There is no need to be so noisy," Katherine said coldly, gathering up the chessmen.

"I've beaten you at last, Kate!"

"Mr. Drew played some part in your victory," she reminded him. "You did not tell us that you were a chess player, Mr. Drew."

"You did not ask me, Miss Spencer. By the by, if you

had moved your king knight from in front of your king you would have prevented the mate."

"Thank you for your advice, Mr. Drew, but I prefer to play my own game."

"You should play against Mr. Drew," Letty said.

"She daren't! She daren't!" Will cried. "Dare you, Kate? He's too good, and she doesn't like being beaten!"

"It is your bedtime, Will."

"No, it isn't!"

"It is. Here is Nurse."

That redoubtable person was indeed waddling purposefully down the staircase in search of her charge, and Will, who had tasted the heady delights of victory, now recognised the reversal of his fortunes. The old woman bore him away, paying not the slightest heed to any protest or argument, and his struggles were rewarded by a sharp cuff round the head.

"Behave yourself, Master William, or I'll be asking Mr. Drew to deal with you."

This threat had its intended effect, and the victor of the chessboard departed meek as a lamb. His sister watched with surprise and increasing irritation. She did not care at all for the sway Mr. Drew held over her brother, nor for the fact that he had apparently won Nurse's wholehearted approval. Taken with Letty's unconcealed admiration for the dandy and Vernon's fawning deference to him, it seemed sometimes that she stood quite alone against the intruder. Well, it only served to harden her resolve: he might win a game of chess— once—but that was all he would win.

Letty had returned reluctantly to her seat and her needlework. Mr. Drew, too, seated himself, and Letty smiled at him brightly.

"Do you sleep soundly at Kielder, Mr. Drew?"

"Very," he replied. "The air suits me."

"The wind does not disturb you? It can make the most dreadful moaning sound sometimes."

"Not at all. I sleep too well."

"I trust you are not afraid of ghosts, Mr. Drew. The castle is said to be haunted, you know."

"I am not at all afraid of ghosts," he answered with a smile. "Which particular ghost do you think might haunt me?"

"Oh, well . . ." Letty blushed, confused. "There is Lady Harriet . . . she is supposed to walk the castle in search of her dead son. Isn't that so, Kate?"

Katherine turned from the armoire where she had been putting away the chess set.

"Kielder is full of shadows from the past, Mr. Drew. Lady Harriet is only one of them."

"Then I hope I shall have the privilege of meeting her one night. It would be an honour," he said mockingly.

"I see you do not really believe in ghosts, Mr. Drew."

"I assure you, Miss Spencer, that I believe in your ghosts as much as I believe in your smoking chimney."

Letty smothered a giggle and bent her head quickly over her needle.

Later, when they had retired upstairs for the night, she voiced the opinion that all their plans would prove useless against Mr. Drew.

"He sees through everything, Kate. He is too clever for us."

"He is not clever at all," Katherine disagreed angrily. "He is odiously conceited and likes to give the impression that he knows everything. He may *say* that he is not afraid of ghosts, but it is quite another thing to feel the same in the middle of the night in a place like Kielder. Why, I am almost afraid of them myself."

"Are you?" Letty said nervously. She looked over her shoulder. The long passageway behind them was very dark. The candle she carried shook in her hand and its flame flickered and nearly died; there was a scuffling sound close by. "What was that?"

"Only a mouse."

"*Only* a mouse! Kate, how can you say that!"

"Surely you are not afraid of mice, Letty. They are so small, and far more frightened of you than you could be of them."

"I am sure that is not true. It could not be. And I am not ashamed to admit it." Miss Lorrimer walked on bravely. "I must say," she continued, "that I do think it would be altogether better if you were not to make it so very clear how much you dislike Mr. Drew."

Miss Spencer stopped dead. "What can you mean by that, Letty? You are not seriously proposing, I hope, that I make myself agreeable to that—to that *dandy*!"

"Not precisely. But—if you think about it, Kate, it would be much cleverer to *seem* a little more friendly towards him. You are so antagonistic all the time that it must arouse his suspicions. Don't you see?"

Katherine considered this for a moment. Then she shook her head. "I do see what you mean, Letty, but I could never bring myself to pretend any friendship for Mr. Drew. Civil I shall be, as well as I am able, but more than that would be impossible."

Letty sighed. "Very well, Kate. But I think it is going to be very difficult to be rid of him. I have a feeling, you see, that he actually *likes* Kielder."

= 4 =

As the days passed it became increasingly apparent that Miss Lorrimer was right. Mr. Drew showed no signs whatever of dissatisfaction. Quite the reverse. He was clearly enjoying himself very much. He went shooting several more times, fished with every success in the river, and, to Miss Spencer's surprise—for she had judged him the kind of man who would never open a book in his life if it could be avoided—spent many hours in the library. His manners and dress were still as elegant as ever, but the air of bored and cynical dissipation which he had worn on his arrival at Kielder had disappeared.

Letty simply could not understand how a gentleman of the *ton* could possibly wish to stay in the castle for a day longer than necessary. She herself was suffering badly. Since Katherine had broken more windowpanes the draughts had multiplied tenfold, and the wind whistled down the passages and moaned about the walls. The hot water was tepid long before it reached the bedchambers and the food was stone cold by the time it was carried up to the dining table. At night, she lay fearfully in a great four-poster bed in which heaven knew how many previous Spencers had slept, and probably died, listening to the scampering of mice and the endless *rattle-rattle* of the shutters. And every creak and groan convinced her that Lady Harriet was abroad and might enter the room at any moment.

Mr. Webber was almost a daily visitor at the castle, as

though he feared that if he neglected to call, some unmentionable fate might befall the two ladies, for whom he considered himself responsible. His awe of Mr. Drew had not eclipsed his awareness that the new owner of Kielder was someone from whom they might be in serious need of protection. Superior knowledge of the world had shown him that London morals were not at all the same as those of Northumberland, although delicacy naturally prevented him from doing other than mutter vague warnings and general expressions of disapproval.

He arrived one morning to find Miss Lorrimer sitting alone in the small parlour beside a miserable fire, and in very low spirits. All his protective instincts were aroused by her woebegone, vulnerable demeanour, and he found himself thinking that there was something rather delightful about a forlorn female who needed taking care of. Katherine, he reflected, did not seem to need taking care of at all—in fact, she had rejected every attempt of his to do so over the past five years. He moved closer and permitted himself to place a comforting hand on Miss Lorrimer's shoulder.

"My dear Letitia, what is the matter?"

"*Everything* is the matter," Letty replied mournfully. "I am heartily sick of Kielder and of being so cold and uncomfortable. How Kate has contrived to live here for so long is beyond understanding. You can have no conception, Vernon, how dreadful it is."

"You should return home at once, Letitia. I told you it was quite unsuitable for you to stay here. Quite unsuitable."

Miss Lorrimer looked up with a shocked expression on her face. "How can you suggest such a thing, Vernon! I should not dream of leaving poor Kate alone. She is my friend—*our* friend—and we must stand by her."

He hastened to retrieve his blunder. "Of course, we must help her all we can. I myself shall do my utmost to do so—if she will let me. I should even stay here, if it were not equally unsuitable and it were not for my chest."

"Your chest? What of your chest?"

"My dear Letitia," he said, pained, "I have often told you that I have a very weak chest. I am extremely susceptible to cold and damp. To stay any length of time at Kielder would undoubtedly be the death of me."

Letty laughed. "Your mama would not let you stay here in any case, Vernon, so you are quite safe." She moved his hand firmly from her shoulder. "And I shall remain."

Mr. Webber walked about the room in some disquiet; his affections had lately undergone another alteration. It had been gradually borne in upon him that Katherine did not, after all, possess quite all the qualities he had lately attributed to her. It was true that her breeding was impeccable, but her obsession with this ramshackle old castle was nothing less than foolish, hotheaded non-sense—as his mother had frequently pointed out. She had displayed a want of propriety over the whole affair that had given him cause for much thought and alarm and led him finally to the conclusion that she might not make such a fitting mistress for Sudley Hall as he had hoped. The matter of Mr. Drew and the dungeon had particularly shocked him. Letitia, on the other hand, might lack breeding, but she was, at least, of a more amenable disposition and more pleasing to the eye—if one overlooked that appalling hair, which, mercifully, would grow out in time. The Unfortunate Connexion, of course, was a grave disadvantage, but money was, after all, money—wherever it came from. The problem was whether his mother could be persuaded to share this charitable view, and Letitia's prolonged stay at the castle in company with an undoubted rake would do nothing to help. He came to a halt beside the fireplace.

"Has Mr. Drew given any hint as to his intentions, Letitia?"

"His intentions?" she said, her blue eyes wide.

"Is he or is he not going to sell Kielder to the family?"

"I really could not say, Vernon. I have formed the impression, though, that he likes it far too well to want to sell it."

"Has Katherine spoken to him again about it?"

"Katherine refuses to speak to him at all beyond the barest civilities."

Mr. Webber drew a deep breath, so that his chest swelled. "Then I shall have to speak with him myself."

Letty looked up in alarm. "I beg you will not, Vernon. You will only make matters worse. And Kate would not like it at all."

"I am more concerned with *you*, my dear Letitia," he said gravely. "You cannot stay at Kielder forever. As I have said, it is most undesirable. So, something must be resolved, and resolved immediately."

He left the room before she could prevent him, and her dismay at the thought of his bumbling intercedence was matched by the awful realisation that she was once again the object of his affections.

Mr. Webber ran his quarry to earth in the library. The room was one of the few in the castle with any degree of comfort. There were good leather chairs, a Turkey carpet, and a fire that burned brightly and well. The walls were lined with an impressive collection of fine volumes acquired over many years by previous baronets. He found Mr. Drew immersed in one of these, seated beside the fire. His entrance made no impression at first upon the reader, who appeared completely absorbed; he was obliged to cough several times and clear his throat loudly before Mr. Drew raised his head.

"What can I do for you, Mr. Webber?"

"My dear sir," he replied, bowing, and wondering as

he did so why his own necktie, so carefully arranged before the glass that morning, did not seem to have quite the same perfection as Mr. Drew's. "I trust you will forgive this intrusion, but there is a matter of the utmost urgency upon which I must speak with you."

Mr. Drew closed his book. "Indeed? Then pray do so at once. I am at your service."

Mr. Webber looked pleased and gratified. "As you may know, sir, I have been acquainted with Miss Spencer and her family for some years. Since her father and her brother died—so *unfortunate*—I have assumed, I like to think, a protective, almost *paternal* role in their affairs."

"So I have observed."

"Then you will have noticed, too, no doubt, that Miss Spencer is inclined to willfulness—regrettable, but understandable. Her father went into a hopeless decline when her mother died; she assumed responsibility for the family and Kielder at a very tender age, since Harry was incapable of doing so. As a consequence, she formed an almost obsessive attachment to this place, quite out of all proportion to its merits."

"I have nothing but admiration for Miss Spencer's attachment to her home and family, Mr. Webber."

"Quite so, quite so," he said hastily. "But you will have seen for yourself that the castle is sadly dilapidated— scarcely more than a ruin—and certainly not a residence fit for any gentleman of consequence, such as yourself."

"I find it charming."

"But you surely do not intend to remain here much longer, sir?"

"For the time being. I am perfectly content."

Mr. Webber wrung his hands. "But can you not see, sir, that the situation is intolerable. Miss Spencer and Miss Lorrimer cannot remain indefinitely under your roof."

"Miss Lorrimer has a home to return to whenever she pleases. Would you prefer that I turn Miss Spencer out on the moors forthwith?"

"No, indeed not. But Miss Lorrimer will not leave Kielder until the matter is settled."

"What matter?"

"Whether or not you will sell Kielder back to the family."

"That, you will forgive my saying, Mr. Webber, is between myself and Miss Spencer."

"Yes, but—"

"Your *paternal* concern for her welfare and that of Miss Lorrimer is most commendable, but quite needless, I assure you. They are both perfectly safe under my roof." Mr. Drew smiled. "I have many bad habits, I admit, but seducing young and innocent women is not one of them."

"I had not thought—"

"I am glad to hear it. So there is no need for us to prolong this discussion any further."

Mr. Drew reopened his book and took up his eyeglass. There was no option for Mr. Webber but to withdraw, and he did so far from comforted and with the unhappy feeling that things were gone beyond his control.

Miss Lorrimer had retreated upstairs to escape from Mr. Webber, and as she made her way down the long passage towards her bedchamber a figure appeared from the door leading to the north tower. Letty gave a shriek of fright and then saw, with relief, that it was Katherine.

"What have you been doing, Kate?"

"I have been up in the tower, Letty, making a hole in the roof."

"Making a hole—Kate, have you gone quite mad?"

"I told you I was going to do it, Letty. There is a window halfway up the tower which overlooks the roof above Mr. Drew's bedchamber. Some of the tiles were already loose, so it was quite easy to dislodge them. I made quite a big hole."

"You mean you *climbed out onto the roof*?"

"How else could I do it?"

"But you might have slipped and fallen! You might have been killed!"

"Oh, the roof is quite flat there. It was easy. And now we must pray for rain—a thunderstorm would be best—and then the water will pour down through the ceiling and, with good fortune, all over Mr. Drew."

"You really do dislike him, don't you, Kate?"

Miss Spencer clenched her fists. "He is not going to take Kielder from us, Letty, if I can help it."

Miss Lorrimer remained upstairs until she was sure that Mr. Webber had left the castle. When eventually she came down she found Mr. Drew standing beside the fire in the great hall with Boots stretched out at his feet. Thinking of the roof tiles, she felt guilty, and the more so when he greeted her pleasantly and with the utmost politeness. He is so handsome, she thought with a sigh, I really do not understand how Kate could have taken him in such dislike. I should forgive him anything.

They talked for a while of London, the subject dearest to Letty's heart, and he answered all her questions patiently, telling her of all those things which she so longed to see for herself.

"If only I could go," she said dejectedly. "My aunt in Kensington is always inviting me to stay with her."

"Then what prevents you?"

"My father does not wish me to go so far away from him—I am his only child, you see—and then, he does not approve very much of my aunt. He says she cares only for silly gossip, which is quite true, as her letters are always full of it, but she is very kindhearted with it. If only I could persuade Kate to come with me, Papa might permit it, for he thinks so highly of her. But she hates the very idea of going. She is prejudiced, you see, against London because of Harry. She thinks it was his undoing."

"Harry was his own undoing. Had he remained in Northumberland he would most likely have come to the same sort of end."

"That is what I am always telling her. But she believes it was the company he kept." Letty blushed suddenly. "I beg your pardon, I did not mean—"

He smiled. "Let us say the company he chose to keep did him no service."

"He already kept bad company here; he spent all his time at the Spencer Arms, gaming and drinking. When he went to London it was worse, I suppose, because there was so much more to tempt him. He left nothing but debts, you know. I have seen poor Kate crying over a mountain of his bills, all to be paid somehow from the little she has left."

"Is that so?" Mr. Drew asked quietly.

Letty looked at him anxiously. "You will not say anything to Kate? She is very proud. She would be so angry if she knew I had spoken about it to you."

"Not one word," he promised.

"If only," said Miss Lorrimer thoughtfully, "she could marry someone very rich, then everything would be solved. But there is only Vernon, and however rich he were she would not marry him."

"Vernon?"

"Mr. Webber. He falls in love with each of us in turn, you see. One month it is Kate, the next me. He has proposed to both of us at least six times, but we always refuse him. Sudley Hall is very pleasant—much nicer than Kielder at any rate, although Kate will never admit it. Except for the east wing, of course, which is the most hideous thing imaginable. But I always think it would be a simple matter to pull it down and rebuild something better."

"Miss Spencer does not strike me as the kind of woman who would marry a house, with or without its east wing," Mr. Drew said, looking amused.

"No, she is not. *Decidedly* not. And then, of course, there is Vernon's mother."

"Ah! He has a mother. How unfortunate."

"She is . . ." Letty searched for the word she wanted. "Very *forceful*—if you understand me."

"Perfectly. I have encountered similar mothers in my time."

"Kate and she do not deal at all well together."

"I rather felt they might not."

"Mrs. Webber tolerates me better, but looks down on me because our money comes from Trade. I am not good enough for her son, you see, despite my inheritance, which would be very useful for rebuilding the east wing. And poor Vernon cannot make up his mind between us!"

"Which one of you has fixed his affections for the present?"

"It *was* Kate—until you arrived. But she has lost favour since then. Vernon thinks she is behaving very foolishly over Kielder. He simply cannot understand why she wants it back at all. And he was very shocked when she wanted to leave you in the dungeon."

"I am indebted to Mr. Webber. I might still be there now."

"Oh, only for just a little while longer," Letty assured him guilelessly. "You must find it excessively boring at Kielder, Mr. Drew."

"Not at all." He smiled. "My visit has been entertaining from the start. It is not every day, after all, that one is incarcerated in a mediaeval dungeon."

"But there is no Society!"

"That is true. But I find that very welcome. I have had

a surfeit of Society, Miss Lorrimer, over the past years. And those years have not been—particularly well spent, shall we say."

"But you will return to London?"

"In time," he answered. "In time."

She searched her mind for something of interest to say. "You spoke of hunting the other day, Mr. Drew. There is a meet at the castle this week, I believe. Shall you join them?"

He was about to reply when, looking up, he saw Miss Spencer coming towards them.

"Mr. Drew would not care for our hunt, Letty. It would be too *rustic* for him, I am sure. Nothing but a pack of farmers who do not mind the mud, and there is nobody who leaves the field until the end of the day."

"I think I might find it amusing," he said languidly. "For a half hour or so. Is there a horse in the stables to suit me, do you think, Miss Spencer?"

"There is Willow," Katherine told him with scorn. "She is old and very reliable and will see you do not get splashed and your leathers spoiled."

"Hmm. What else?"

"Or there is Kestrel. But I do not advise him as a mount for you, Mr. Drew. I doubt you would be able to stop him when your half hour or so is up."

"He sounds more to my taste nonetheless. I prefer to be at the front of the field rather than the back, you see." He smiled at her. "That way I shall stay clear of the mud *and* the farmers."

The day of the hunt was dull, cold, and windy. Letty remained indoors and watched from the window as they moved off from the courtyard below, clattering out noisily across the drawbridge onto the bleak moorland. Mr. Drew was mounted on Kestrel, a big-boned, fiery bay who had once belonged to Harry Spencer. Katherine was on her chestnut mare. Both, Letty observed, were up in the forefront of the field. She watched them until they were out of sight and only the distant sound of the horn could be heard.

For Katherine, the exhilaration of hunting lay in the chase itself—the soaring high over stone walls, the galloping at full tilt across the wild and beautiful Northumberland countryside. She did not like the finish, and although she told herself many times that foxes were pests and a menace to the farmers' livelihood, the best day's hunting, for her, was a day when they did not kill at all.

To begin with, she addressed herself entirely to the task of keeping up in the front of the field. Later, she began to look about for Mr. Drew, thinking that he had probably already turned for home, since the conditions were so bad. The terrain would be unfamiliar to him. Instead of the soft, brush hedges of the South there were hard stone walls to contend with, and rough, uneven ground. She was surprised and annoyed, therefore, to discover him suddenly alongside her, seated astride Harry's great brute of a horse with every appearance of ease. Her late brother had scarcely been able to control the beast, and the bay had constantly made a nuisance of himself on the hunting field, charging ahead of the master and jumping wildly across others' paths. But Kestrel was evidently in a strangely docile mood, taking his jumps perfectly and keeping an even pace with the leaders. Katherine set her chestnut at a wall; the mare responded willingly but stumbled badly on landing, so that she lost ground. Out of the corner of her eye, Katherine saw the bay sail over and gallop on past her.

Try as she might, she could not catch up with Mr. Drew again. Her chestnut was no match for the big horse striding out with faultless rhythm. As Mr. Drew had pointed out, to be anywhere but the front of the field meant being constantly showered with mud, and Katherine's temper was not improved by the suspicion that a good deal of the mud that came her way was thrown up by Kestrel's flying hooves.

A few fields later they lost the scent, and waited while hounds were drawing again. Spots of rain were beginning to fall, and banks of black storm clouds were building up on the far horizon. Katherine thought of the hole in the roof and felt a little better. Not everything, after all, was going to go Mr. Drew's way. He brought his horse alongside her, and she saw with satisfaction that he was by no means unmuddied.

"I thought you would have gone home by now," she remarked. "Your half hour or so is long past."

"Oh, I have decided to stay a while longer; I am quite enjoying myself."

She turned her head towards him. "What about the mud?" she enquired sarcastically.

"Do you mean the mud on your right cheek?" he asked. "Let me remove it for you."

He leaned forward from the saddle, proffering his handkerchief; she saw the laughter in his blue eyes and knew that he had been mocking her all the time. The dandy could ride to hounds just as well as he could shoot and fish, and all talk of going home after the first few fields to spare his clothes a muddying had been nonsensical rubbish, deliberately said to hoodwink her. She tried to think of some crushing remark to set him down as he deserved, but before the right one could come to her, hounds had found again in the covert and the huntsman's horn blew Gone Away.

The mare had recovered her wind and now took her place close behind the leaders. To Katherine's irritation, however, Mr. Drew remained alongside, so that they galloped stride for stride and took their jumps together. She had the galling impression that he was actually holding back his horse to her pace. There was little point, though, in saying anything, as the wind would have carried any words away; she set herself instead to draw free of him, urging her mount on still faster. It was raining in earnest now and she blinked to see more clearly. Hounds were in full cry, streaming in a baying pack across the field ahead, and the pink of the huntsmen's coats made bright splashes against the dullness of winter. She caught a sudden glimpse of the fox two fields further on—a red-brown streak running over the sheep-cropped turf, fleeing for its life. She shut her eyes for a moment and prayed that he would get away.

When she opened them again the next stone wall was nearer and higher than she had expected. She collected the mare quickly and put her straight at the jump. The chestnut rose gallantly into the air but hit the top of the wall with her forelegs and fell heavily on the far side. Katherine was thrown from the saddle into the path of the following riders.

Curiously, she felt nothing. There was no pain and very little sound. The world had receded from her to nothing more than a faint tremor of thundering hooves and the wetness of the rain upon her face. There was a murmur of voices somewhere near; someone loosened her cravat and gently wiped her face; she felt herself lifted from the ground and carried. Then she remembered nothing more.

— 5 —

"I know you will not wish to hear this, Kate, but I am going to tell you just the same. Mr. Drew was quite wonderfully behaved. They say he simply *flung* himself off Kestrel to shield you from the other horses. You might have been trampled to death! And it was he, you know, who carried you all the way back across *three* fields, until they could put you in Farmer Thorpe's cart and bring you the rest of the way home. And I'm sure I do not know how he managed to carry you so far, for you must be fairly heavy, being so tall, although he made very light of it." Letty paused and settled herself more comfortably on the end of Katherine's bed. "Everyone was very worried because you had fallen so hard; it was very fortunate that it was no worse than a little concussion and a bruised ankle. Mr. Drew was—"

"Letty, will you please stop talking about Mr. Drew. I do not wish to hear any more of him. I am very grateful to him, of course, for coming so quickly to my aid, but I am sure it is no more than anyone would have done. He happened to be the nearest person." Miss Spencer put her hand to her head, which was aching intolerably. "All that matters is that my horse was not hurt badly, for it was all my fault that she fell. If I had been paying proper attention instead of worrying about the poor fox it would never have happened."

"Well, you need not worry about the fox," Letty said with a laugh, "for I hear that it got away."

"I'm so glad."

"You will be glad about something else, I daresay. During the thunderstorm last night the ceiling came down in Mr. Drew's bedchamber."

"What!" Miss Spencer sat bolt upright, wincing at the sudden pain in her head. "It really came down?"

"Well, not quite the whole ceiling, but a big piece of it. It rained all night, you know—although you would not have noticed—and the water poured through the roof where you had taken the tiles away and brought down all the plaster. I must say, Kate, that it was a poor reward for Mr. Drew, after all he did for you. Just think, he carried you all that way, lugging you like a sack of potatoes, only to have the ceiling come down on him in the middle of the night! I declare I could not meet his eye this morning, for I am certain he knew very well it was no accident."

Miss Spencer was silent for a moment. Then she said, "You are being too softhearted, Letty. I, for one, am delighted the ceiling fell down. I meant it to happen. I hope Mr. Drew got wet."

"He has asked after you several times already today," Miss Lorrimer said accusingly.

Miss Spencer shrugged.

"And Vernon called this morning. He was most upset. Really *quite* distraught! Beware, Kate! I do believe that your little accident has quite restored you to favour in his eyes!"

Nurse, entering at that moment, despatched the visitor summarily. "Out of here, this minute! A week's rest and quiet was what the doctor said, and a week's rest and quiet is what Miss Katherine's going to have!"

Letty ran off, laughing, and Nurse fussed and grumbled round the bed, straightening covers and plumping pillows, as she had done when Katherine was a child. There was an odd hammering sound in Miss Spencer's head—or at least she imagined it to be in her head, until she realised that it was coming instead from somewhere in the castle.

"What is that noise, Nurse? All that hammering?"

"Och, they're mending the roof. Some tiles blew off in the storm and the ceiling came down in Mr. Drew's room. The place is falling to bits about our heads! There's an army been set to mend all the windows, too, and a pretty penny *that'll* cost him! The man's daft to trouble himself. If I were him I'd let it fall down the rest of the way. It's nothing but an old ruin!"

"It isn't to me."

"Aye, I know that full well, lassie. You're blind as a bat about it. It's more than you could manage to keep Kielder in one piece. You're lucky Mr. Drew has happened along to do it for you, Katherine Spencer. Just you remember that!"

After four days Miss Spencer had had more than enough of being idle in bed. She was bored, and felt quite recovered, although her ankle still hurt when she tried to walk. The ennui of lying with nothing to do had been aggravated by the sounds that reached her of everyone else's activity: Letty laughing, Will shouting, Boots barking, and the banging and hammering of the workmen. She decided to investigate, and defying Nurse, dressed herself and made a tour of the castle, limping along with the aid of a stick.

At least twenty men had been set to work, repairing not only the great hole in the ceiling of Mr. Drew's bedchamber but also every broken windowpane, every rotted shutter, every decayed floorboard. Miss Spencer stood and stared, and whilst she was doing so, Mr. Drew spoke behind her.

"You are quite recovered, I hope, Miss Spencer?"

She turned. "Quite recovered, thank you, Mr. Drew."

"But your ankle is not better yet?"

"No, but it will be very soon."

"I hope you are right. There are no other ill effects from your fall?"

"None." She hesitated. "I believe I have to thank you for coming to my aid so promptly, Mr. Drew."

"There is nothing to thank me for."

She was determined to be fair. "But for you I might have been trampled."

"Unlikely. Horses always avoid doing that if they possibly can."

"And . . . and you carried me across three fields—or so Letty says. I am afraid I am no lightweight."

He said, smiling, "I did not find you particularly heavy."

"But you must have become very muddy," she said, eyeing him. "How dreadful for you!"

"Mud can be removed, fortunately," he answered.

"It was fortunate, too, for me that you stayed so long with the hunt."

"Yes, wasn't it?" he said blandly. "Tell me, are you satisfied with the work being done presently?"

"Kielder belongs to you, Mr. Drew. It is not for me to say."

"Nonetheless, I should value your opinion. The dining room is particularly improved. Would you care to inspect it?"

"If you insist."

"Will you take my arm?"

"Thank you, but this stick serves me very well."

The dry rot that had plagued the corner of the dining room for many years had been removed and fresh boards laid; already the dreadful musty smell had faded, and the room seemed to have taken on a new elegance and comfort. The same might be said of the whole of Kielder. There were still plenty of draughts, but it was warmer, drier, and infinitely more pleasant.

"All this will cost you a great deal, Mr. Drew."

"The repairs were necessary. Besides, I have a party

from London arriving in a few days time, and they might have found the rigours of Kielder somewhat trying, don't you think?"

"Very likely," she responded coolly. "Hothouse plants from the South do not thrive this far north, Mr. Drew. How many will your party be?"

"No more than five. Two married ladies with their husbands and a Mr. Lovell, an old friend of mine from school days. They are very curious to see Kielder. You have no objection?"

"I can have no objection, Mr. Drew, since you are presently the owner of Kielder. When will you give me your decision?"

"My decision, Miss Spencer?"

"You know very well what I mean. When will you decide whether or not you are going to sell Kielder back to our family?" She bit her lip. "I suppose, with all these repairs and expenses, you will naturally expect a higher price."

"I have not yet made up my mind," he said. "So I cannot give you your answer."

"But surely you must have some idea," she cried. "Some inkling whether you wish to stay."

"I shall tell you that by the end of this month."

"Not before?"

"Not before."

She shrugged. "Very well."

"And until then," he said levelly, "let us declare a truce, Miss Spencer."

"A truce?"

"Now it is you who are pretending that you do not know what I mean. You will never succeed in smoking me out of Kielder, Miss Spencer, or flushing me out either. Or inducing me to leave by any means whatever. The more you try, the more determined I am to remain. Do you understand? So let us declare a truce between us. What do you say?"

She raised her eyes to his face. Behind the charming manners and good looks there was a hardness which warned her that she would be wise to concede temporary defeat.

"Agreed, Mr. Drew," she said reluctantly. "A truce."

6

THE NEWS OF the impending arrival of the party from London threw Miss Lorrimer into a state of panic. She reviewed her wardrobe again and again, and each time with increasing despair and dissatisfaction.

"I shall not be able to hold my head up," she told Katherine dejectedly, "when everything I possess must be out of fashion. How they will laugh! What a country dowd I shall be taken for! Look at this gown, Kate . . . everything is wrong about it: the sleeves, the neckline, the hem—all out of date and ridiculous! I have not a single—" She stopped suddenly in midsentence and covered her mouth with her hand. "Kate! My hair! I had quite forgot! What will they think of my hair? Nobody is wearing theirs *à la* Titus anymore. Oh, I shall die of mortification!"

"Don't be silly, Letty. Let them think what they like. What does it matter?"

"It is all very well for you, Kate, but you do not care in the least how you look. It is nothing to you that your gown is ten years out of fashion at the very least!"

"Nothing whatever."

"But supposing they are very grand. Supposing they look down their noses at us? Kate! Supposing they discover my Connexion with *Trade*!"

As Mr. Drew had promised, the party from London were five in number: Mr. and Mrs. de Vere, Lord and Lady Beverly, and Mr. Lovell. At first sight, Miss

Lorrimer's worst fears seemed realised. They were, all five, greatly superior in appearance and style; their clothes of the first stare and quality, their manners languidly elegant, as befits those with nothing more arduous to trouble themselves about than the pursuit of their own pleasure.

On closer acquaintance, however, it was discovered that there were differences: Mrs. de Vere was quite as haughty and unpleasant as she looked, whilst her husband had very little to say for himself and spent most of his time dozing by the fire; Lord Beverly was both pompous and boring, and his wife, who was a beauty, coupled arrogance with insolence. Only Mr. Lovell proved agreeable. He was young, smiling, and anxious to please. Presented to Miss Spencer, he bowed low over her hand and seemed unable to conceal his surprise at her appearance, exchanging several glances with Mr. Drew. Katherine concluded that it was her unfashionable dress which had caused such amazement. His introduction to Letty, however, produced such obvious admiration that Miss Lorrimer instantly forgot her fears about either her gown or her hair. Except for Mr. Drew, she thought she had never seen a more handsome or charming gentleman.

Lady Beverly, in the manner of her kind, lost no time in establishing her position of authority and excellence, as well as her superiority to the rest of the ladies present. On arrival, she had scrutinised both Miss Spencer and Miss Lorrimer minutely and been quickly satisfied that neither had the remotest claim to rival herself. Miss Spencer she had regarded with an odd mixture of amusement and curiosity; Miss Lorrimer had been dismissed with careless contempt. She had not been in the castle for more than five minutes before she was exclaiming over the coldness and discomfort, the interminable distance from London, the lack of any refinements, the whole barbarous nature of the North, and with it all, her conviction that Mr. Drew would not support it for much longer and would surely return soon to the South.

"It pains me to have to contradict you, my dear Laura," Mr. Drew said pleasantly, "but I rather like the North."

"Impossible, Richard! I know you are teasing me! You always tease. How could someone like yourself find it anything but excruciatingly dull. To be so far from London, deprived of all Society and amusement! How you must hate it!"

"It seems to suit him very well," Mr. Lovell commented drily. "I have never seen you in better health, Richard. Or better spirits."

"Can't abide the North myself," offered Lord Beverly, who had taken up the best position before the fire and was warming himself comfortably. His considerable bulk took most of the heat from the rest of the company. "Rum sort of place, to my mind. Very different from the South."

"That is exactly what I was just saying, George," his wife said impatiently. "One would scarcely know one was still in England up here."

"We are not savages, Lady Beverly," Katherine said indignantly.

Her ladyship gave a little, pitying smile. "Are you acquainted at all with the South, Miss Spencer?"

"No."

"You have *never* been to London?"

"Never."

"Then you cannot understand what I mean."

"Of course she cannot," agreed Mrs. de Vere.

"I know enough of London to understand that there are more savages there than in Northumberland," Miss Spencer replied. "To live in a city does not necessarily render a person civilised. The humblest ploughman may be more truly refined than a city dweller, in my opinion."

Lady Beverly looked towards Mr. Drew. "I am well

set down, am I not, Richard? Miss Spencer does not, I collect, take kindly to us wicked city folk!"

"Perhaps with good reason," he replied.

And Katherine had the satisfaction of seeing her ladyship flush and look discomforted.

"What's the shooting like?" Lord Beverly enquired, rocking to and fro on his heels perilously close to Boots's feathery tail. The spaniel, who had been edged out of his customary place, raised his head reproachfully. "Fond of a good day's shooting, you know."

"I can promise you an excellent bag, George, providing you hold the gun straight, for once."

"He's the worst shot in England," Mr. Lovell whispered in Letty's ear.

Mrs. de Vere prodded her husband in the ribs to waken him. "Do you hear that, Jack? The shooting's good, so I suppose that's one thing to be thankful for."

Mr. de Vere, however, only grunted, before falling back asleep again. His wife looked at him with irritation, but decided to leave well alone. "The journey has exhausted him," she explained. "All those miles and miles . . . I had no idea that England was so *long*."

As though to prevent further discussion on the distance between North and South, Mr. Lovell intervened quickly to enquire from Miss Spencer as to the history of Kielder. "It is very old, is it not? I recall Harry speaking of it. . . ." He coloured, realising this was an unfortunate subject, but Katherine was grateful to him for his obviously good intentions, and obliged by recounting a short summary of the castle's story. Mr. de Vere snored gently, Lady Beverly fidgeted with her shawl, Lord Beverly yawned, and Mrs. de Vere looked about her. Mr. Drew watched Miss Spencer.

"Are there dungeons?" Mr. Lovell asked.

It was Miss Spencer's turn to blush, seeing Mr. Drew's eye upon her. "There is one."

"Were prisoners kept there?"

"Until quite recently," Mr. Drew said. "Isn't that so, Miss Spencer? But you have not told them of Lady Harriet."

"And who is Lady Harriet?" demanded Lady Beverly, suspicious of a possible rival.

"The castle ghost, my dear Laura," Mr. Drew informed her. "Her portrait hangs in the long gallery. I suggest you study it with care in case you meet her. She walks the castle at night in search of her dead baby son. A very sad tale."

Mrs. de Vere glanced over her shoulder into the shadows of the great hall. "Do you mean to say that you have seen this—this apparition yourself, Richard?"

"Not as yet, Caroline. But I have little doubt that I shall—eventually."

"Queer sort of things, ghosts," Lord Beverly said thoughtfully. "Don't know that I believe in them myself. Still—there's a lot of 'em about, you know. Charlie Rutledge has one at his place, I b'lieve. Frightens everyone silly. Some fellow walking about with his head under his arm. The ladies don't like it at all."

"Well, *I* do not believe a word of it," Lady Beverly cried. "The whole idea is utter nonsense! Nor do you, Richard. You are far too cynical to believe in fairy stories!"

"Spoke to someone who'd seen this fellow," her husband persisted doggedly. "Swears he did. Dressed in doublet and hose and carrying his head."

"Whoever *that* was had doubtless dined too well," her ladyship remarked acidly. "Don't you agree, Richard?"

"Oh, every self-respecting ancestral home must have its ghost," he replied, smiling.

"Do not tell me there is one at Cheynings. For if so, I have never heard you speak of it."

He frowned. Mrs. de Vere nudged her friend sharply in the ribs, and, to Miss Spencer's surprise, Lady Beverly fell suddenly silent.

Later, when Katherine and Letty were alone upstairs, they discussed the visitors.

"I do not know when I have met such an unpleasant creature as Lady Beverly," Miss Lorrimer declared. "She may be a great beauty and all that is fashionable, but you are quite right, Kate, that is not everything. She cannot open her mouth without complaining of something, and I did not care for her manner towards you one bit. Mrs. de Vere is no better. I do not know what her husband is like, since he is always asleep, but Lord Beverly cannot put a proper sentence together—*and* he takes all the fire from everyone else. I own I am greatly disappointed in Mr. Drew's friends from London. Except for Mr. Lovell." Letty sighed happily. "*He* is most agreeable and very kind, I think. And is he not handsome, Kate? He is almost as handsome as Mr. Drew. Not quite as wonderfully dressed, of course, nor of quite such consequence, perhaps, but to my mind he is more *comfortable* to know. There is something about Mr. Drew that is just a little *frightening*."

"There is something about Mr. Drew that is very strange," Katherine retorted. "Did you not notice, Letty, how they all kept nodding and winking at each other as though there were some secret joke? And when Lady Beverly asked Mr. Drew whether he had a ghost at somewhere called Cheynings, Mrs. de Vere behaved as though she had said something very wrong."

"Lady Beverly always says something very wrong. And what is Cheynings?"

"Mr. Drew's country home, I suppose." Katherine shook her head. "There is some mystery, I am sure of it."

"The mystery to me is how Mr. Drew could care anything for someone like Lady Beverly. It is plain, though, that *she* cares for him. Have you remarked, Kate, how she *flirts* with him? If Lord Beverly were not such a dry stick I should almost feel sorry for him, having such a wife."

"She does not believe in ghosts, Letty, did you hear?" Katherine smiled. "I have a mind to teach her ladyship a lesson."

"You mean—you mean Lady Harriet?"

"What else? Tomorrow night, I think, or perhaps the night after. We shall see."

Downstairs beside the dying fire in the great hall, Mr. Drew and Mr. Lovell were also engaged in a private conversation, the remainder of the party having retired for the night. They sat drinking brandy whilst the candles burned low.

"Damn it, Richard, you might have warned me," Mr. Lovell said. "She's not at all as Harry would have had us believe. I was never more deceived in my life! I pictured some dragon breathing fire and brimstone at us across the drawbridge. Instead I find Miss Spencer—no more than twenty-two or -three, and if not quite a beauty, certainly no dragon!"

"I do warn you, though, David, that she has fiery qualities."

"Oh, I can see that she is a woman of spirit. I admire her for that. I liked the way she set Laura down! Why in heaven's name did you invite those four here, by the by? You know you can't support 'em, and neither can I."

"I didn't invite them. They insisted on coming, out of vulgar curiosity and boredom. They have nothing better to do at this time of year, as you know. They are desperate for amusement—*any* amusement—and they hoped they might find it here at Kielder." Mr. Drew smiled. "I let them come, my dear David, because they will be sorely disappointed and because the bracing air of the North and the appalling discomforts of Kielder will do them all the world of good. As they have done me."

"I must say, you seem a reformed character. Look at you!" Mr. Lovell laughed. "Sober, abstemious, well behaved . . . I can hardly believe it! I have never known an evening when you were not roaring drunk and spoiling for trouble. It is incredible! One of the most disreputable rakes in London comporting himself with all the decorum of a country parson! Has Miss Spencer any notion of the hell-raiser she is nurturing in her bosom?"

"That hardly seems an apt description of Miss Spencer's attitude towards me," Mr. Drew said drily.

"No, I could see she don't like you. She don't toadeat you like all the rest. The more I learn of Miss Spencer, the more I approve her good sense. Unlike most of the unmarried ladies in London, she is not grovelling at your feet. What a change that must be for you, Richard!" Mr. Lovell drained his glass. "Dash it, this is an awkward business! What's to be done about it? If I'd known . . . If I'd realised what she was really like, I should never have made such a bet. We were all foxed, though, and it seemed good sport at the time. But now, I'm not so sure . . . Let's call it off. Tell her the truth."

"A wager is a wager, David. To the end of the month, I believe we said."

"I don't care for it," Mr. Lovell said worriedly.

His companion rose to refill their glasses. "There is no need to look so anxious. In essence it *is* the truth. And Miss Spencer is not yet in a decline, I assure you. On the contrary, since I first set foot in this ruin of a castle she has been most happily and gainfully employed in trying every means she can think of, fair or foul, to be rid of me. Mostly foul."

"Really?" Mr. Lovell looked fascinated. "What has she done? Do tell me?"

"To begin with, she locked me in the dungeon."

"Good God!"

"Or rather, her small brother did. But Miss Spencer was all in favour, it seems, of my remaining there indefinitely—or at least, presumably, until I had agreed to sell Kielder back to her, as she wants me to do.

Without the intervention of a neighbour who happened to be visiting, I might be incarcerated down there yet!"

Mr. Lovell stared, and then roared with laughter. "Great heavens! She certainly don't like you at all! What else?"

"Her plan has been to render Kielder even more uninhabitable than it was already. She broke every pane of glass that remained, so that the place leaked like a sieve. As this did not appear to disturb me unduly, she removed some tiles from the roof above my bedroom so that the rain brought the ceiling down on me in the middle of the night."

Mr. Lovell shook his head wonderingly. "What resource! What spirit! My admiration for her grows and grows."

"Oh, I have had my revenge, in small ways," Mr. Drew said with a smile. He prodded the sleeping Boots gently with the toe of his shoe. "She offered me this lazy, untrained hound as a perfect gun dog, hoping to make a complete fool of me. Naturally, he frightened all the game, barking and running all over the place."

"If she'd known you were one of the best shots in the country, she'd have thought of something different," Mr. Lovell commented, disappointed.

"I had the devil's own job to hit anything at first, I can tell you. Until I'd brought the dog to heel."

"Well, I don't fancy you'll bring Miss Spencer to heel so easy." Mr. Lovell drank deeply from his glass and stretched his long legs towards the fire contentedly. He had quite recovered his naturally buoyant spirits. "Tell you what, Richard. Twenty guineas you can't make her fall in love with you by the time the month's up. And you're a fool if you take me on—though I could do with the money."

"Make it thirty guineas."

"Spoken like the true and evil gambler you are at

heart! Very well, thirty guineas. But you're bound to lose. Can't help it. She can't abide you. Not even *your* charm can work this one, Richard. You might as well give me the money now."

"We shall see."

"No chance, my dear fellow." Mr. Lovell squinted into his nearly empty glass. "This brandy is damnably good, I say. Excellent cellars here, though the rest of the place is ramshackle as hell."

"You should have been here before I had all the windows repaired."

Mr. Lovell shuddered. "Couldn't stand it here for very long myself. If it weren't for one *particular* advantage to the place, I think I'd be off again tomorrow."

"I take it you are referring to Miss Lorrimer?"

"You saw me admiring her? Well, she's enchanting. Enchanting! That terrible hair! That disastrous gown! That bewitching smile! Damn it, Richard, I've never met anyone quite like her!"

"Miss Lorrimer does indeed have some claim to being unique," Mr. Drew agreed, amused. "She is also the only child of a wealthy widower and likely to inherit a substantial fortune of her own. From Trade, I believe."

Mr. Lovell looked suddenly downcast. "Oh, dear!"

"Don't tell me you are squeamish about such a connexion, David."

"Of course not! Who cares about such things? It does not make Miss Lorrimer one wit less adorable."

"Well, then?"

"You know my scruples, Richard. A younger son with little money and no prospects pursuing a little provincial heiress . . . why, I should be thought a barefaced fortune hunter. And *that* I could not abide!"

"Don't be absurd, David. If you like her, what does it matter what others think?"

The other shook his head. "It's no use. Anyway, if she

is an heiress, I daresay there must be a string of suitors after her already."

"I can see you do not know Northumberland well. There is only one—my noble deliverer from the dungeon—and I think you may safely disregard him as a serious contender."

Mr. Lovell sighed morosely. "Being a younger son is a confounded nuisance. You have no idea how lucky you are, Richard."

"There are some disadvantages."

"You mean all those matchmaking mamas thrusting their beautiful daughters into your arms. *I* should not mind it. Oh, well . . ." Mr. Lovell cheered up again quickly, as was his way. "At least I shall win thirty guineas at the end of this month."

"But lose fifty."

"Don't be too sure, Richard. I have a feeling that for once, I may take all."

7

THE FULL HORROR of the deficiencies of Kielder soon became apparent to the visitors from London. Lady Beverly's first impressions were found to have all too solid a foundation: cold food, cold water, and cold draughts—despite the new windows—did nothing to improve her opinion of the North nor the sweetness of her temper. And Mrs. de Vere echoed every grumble and complaint. The invasion of the castle had thrown an impossible strain upon Purves, who, with his depleted staff and his own frail strength, was quite unable to meet the demands of the situation. Rather deaf and very shortsighted, he frequently failed either to see or to hear what was commanded or required of him. Fortunately, his deafness also meant that many of the acid comments made went unheard too. To make matters worse, it snowed.

It had begun with a few flakes drifting down as light as goose feathers. Within an hour there was a blizzard blowing round the castle, and within two the snow was lying thick and white across the moors. Plans that the party were forming for returning to London had to be abandoned, as it became clear that a long journey would now be out of the question.

Mr. Drew being nowhere to be found, Lady Beverly had worked herself into a frenzy of frustration and boredom, when unexpectedly, amusement offered itself to her in the shape of Mr. Webber, who had coaxed his horse through the snow all the way from Sudley Hall and arrived triumphantly at the castle, anxious to make the acquaintance of the visitors. The *haut ton*, he had been informed, did not necessarily behave any better than others of a lower station: in fact, it was whispered that they frequently behaved very much worse. He mounted the stairs to the great hall in Purves's wake, therefore, half expecting to find an orgy in progress.

He discovered, instead, a circle of strangers sitting round the fireside, trying to keep warm. Miss Spencer, he saw, was absent, and so was Mr. Drew, but Miss Lorrimer was amongst the group and was, Mr. Webber noted with disapproval, seated next to a young man and talking to him with every sign of enjoyment. As he approached, all conversation ceased and every head turned towards him.

Mr. Webber was immediately struck by the superiority of the party. He was quite dazzled by the beauty of Lady Beverly, who, as she did for all strange gentlemen of whatever description until she could establish whether or not they merited it, favoured him with a gracious smile. The haughty mien of Mrs. de Vere impressed him deeply, and Lord Beverly needed only his title to recommend him. Mr. de Vere was asleep but still looked the perfect gentleman. Mr. Lovell he considered to have a rather frivolous air about him, and he was surprised and grieved that Letitia should, apparently, find him such congenial company. The general conversation, though, proved very much to his taste.

"That coat you are wearing, Mr. Webber," cried Lady Beverly, clasping her hands ecstatically before her. "I am all admiration, all praise for one who could contrive such cut, such elegance, so far from London! It could only have come from Mr. Weston or Stultz. Do tell me which one?"

Mr. Webber turned pink with pleasure and patted the lapels of his country-tailored coat. The names meant nothing to him, but he grasped something of their significance.

"Indeed, do you think so, ma'am?"

"Oh, *yes*! Do you not agree, George? Have you *ever* seen such tailoring?"

Lord Beverly, who had not, had already observed with some amazement the lumpish padding in the shoulders of Mr. Webber's upper garment, and its distressing fit elsewhere, but he was not an unkind man and contented himself with a noncommittal grunt as he toasted himself before the fire. He spread his legs a little wider and shifted Boots another quarter of an inch from the blaze.

"I must correct your ladyship," Mr. Webber averred modestly. "This coat was fashioned by a tailor not ten miles from here, and not in London at all!"

Lady Beverly clapped her hands. "I do not believe it! You are jesting! Those shoulders could not have come from anywhere but London!"

"Indeed, they did not, ma'am."

"But, of course, it is the figure that wears the coat that makes or mars it. Is that not so, Caroline?"

"Oh, certainly!"

The two ladies exchanged sly looks. Mr. Webber, however, noticed nothing. He was too busy drawing in his stomach and affecting a nonchalant stance before Lady Beverly.

"You are too kind. But I fear our country style must strike you as sadly unmodish."

"Not at all, Mr. Webber! Miss Spencer has assured me several times that there is quite as much refinement in Northumberland as in London, and now that I have met you I am quite ready to believe it. Do tell me, what do you call that wonderful arrangement of your cravat? It is all that is elegant!"

Mr. Webber fingered his neckwear in wonder. It was true that he had taken extra pains with his appearance before setting out on this visit, but in all his life, nobody had ever before described him as elegant. He stole a surreptitious look at himself in the looking glass nearby and concluded that he did indeed cut rather a fine figure.

"I—er, don't have a name for it, ma'am. It is nothing but my own way—"

"Do you hear that, Beverly? It is all Mr. Webber's own invention! My husband will spend an hour or more trying to tie his neckcloth in all kinds of arrangements. How long do you take with yours?"

"Not above ten minutes, I think."

"*Ten minutes!* Is that all? Mr. Webber, you are beyond belief! You must show us all your secret! How do you contrive to tie your cravat so exquisitely in ten minutes!"

In another moment Mr. Webber, flushed with pride and pleasure, would have shown her then and there, if Mr. Lovell had not intervened to spoil the sport. He adroitly changed the conversation, and in doing so drew much of the fire onto himself. This earned him Miss Lorrimer's warm gratitude, for although she was not above teasing Mr. Webber herself at times, she did not care to see him being used so cruelly.

Miss Spencer, having eschewed the company of the visitors and being unaware of Mr. Webber's visit, was enjoying the peace and quiet of the library, where she had gone to choose a book. She selected a volume from the shelves and was turning the pages with interest when a slight sound behind her made her start and turn.

Mr. Drew was sitting in one of the high-backed leather chairs, a book open on his knee. At once she prepared to retreat, but he lowered his glass and said indifferently, "Pray do not heed me, Miss Spencer. I shall not disturb you, and you do not disturb me, I promise. I imagine we are both in search of tranquillity."

She still could not reconcile the dandy and his frivolous elegance with the scholarly reader she knew him to be.

"There is little enough of *that* to be found presently at Kielder," she replied. "Your London friends are far from tranquil."

"You do not care for them?"

"Since you ask—not at all. Except for Mr. Lovell, who seems very pleasant."

"Mr. Lovell is indeed a charming fellow. *He* may be termed a friend—the rest are mere acquaintances."

"Whatever their standing, I wish they would not stay much longer."

"Unfortunately, the snow is holding them prisoner as effectively as if you had locked them up in your dungeon, Miss Spencer."

She coloured, but said spiritedly, "*Unfortunately*, Mr. Drew? Surely *you* do not want them to leave? To have friends—or even acquaintances—of such wit and fashion to entertain you now must be a most welcome state of affairs. Lady Beverly, particularly, seems intent on pleasing you. And she is a great beauty."

"That remark shows how little you know me, Miss Spencer. Odd though it may seem to you, I find great beauty, as you call it, rather boring. I have found that the most pleasing women invariably have little claim to beauty. That is not to say that I do not admire it, but that I do not prize it above other qualities. You yourself, after all, do not allow good looks in the opposite sex to prejudice you in favour—"

"That is different."

"How so?"

"Good looks in a woman are generally considered desirable."

"But not in a man?"

Miss Spencer felt the ground uncertain beneath her and sought safety in a change of direction. "The mystery is how her ladyship ever came to marry Lord Beverly. He must be twice her age."

"Money," replied Mr. Drew. "There is no mystery.

Beverly is a rich man, and Laura came from a family of six daughters. It must be one of the few sensible things she has ever done in her life."

"You are very cynical, Mr. Drew. And I do not call marrying for money necessarily at all sensible—especially if it means having a husband like Lord Beverly."

Mr. Drew smiled. "You, I collect, would never marry for money, then?"

"No, I should not."

"Not even to save Kielder?"

There was the smallest hesitation. "Not even to save Kielder."

"You believe then," he said, "in marrying only for love?"

"I think so."

"Lady Beverly would consider that very provincial of you, Miss Spencer."

"I daresay." She moved towards the door.

"Do not let me drive you away."

"I shall never let you drive me away, Mr. Drew."

He looked down at the book on his knee. "The library at Kielder is as excellent as the cellar, and equally worth sampling."

"I have known that since a child," she responded. "My father encouraged me to read as much as I wanted."

"Then you are indebted to him."

"Yes, I am." She paused. "Did you have a similarly disposed parent, Mr. Drew?"

"My father, fortunately, is still living. Yes, he has encouraged me in all intellectual pursuits. I fear, though, that I have proved a great disappointment to him, and to my tutors. Too little of my time has been spent in the library and too much at the gaming table—and elsewhere." He looked at her. "He would approve of *you*, Miss Spencer. Of that there can be no doubt."

"It seems unlikely that we shall ever meet."

"Unlikely. But not impossible."

She searched her mind for other questions that might reveal something of his background.

"Do you have a library at Cheynings, Mr. Drew?"

She thought he started, but could not be sure, for he answered her quite matter-of-factly: "There is one. Almost the match of this."

"And where is your country home?"

"In the South."

"Where, precisely?"

"The Southwest . . . precisely."

Katherine saw that he would not be drawn upon the subject, and was more than ever convinced that there was some mystery about him.

The snow continued to fall, and by dark, lay deep around the castle, blanketing all with uniform whiteness. Mr. Webber, who had enjoyed his visit exceedingly and found the visitors altogether delightful, had quite failed to notice the passing of time or the deterioration in the weather and was consequently unable to return home to Sudley Hall. As Miss Spencer remarked bitterly to Miss Lorrimer, it was bad enough being snowed in with Lady Beverly and the others without having Vernon to contend with as well.

"And," added Letty in some distress, "they will tease him unmercifully, although he is unaware of it—which makes it worse, somehow. He has been the butt of all their stupid jokes."

"Poor Vernon!"

"Mr. Lovell will do everything he can to stop them," Letty assured Katherine. "*He* is everything that is good and kind."

"I am sure that he is." Miss Spencer was rummaging in an old oak chest. "It is high time for me to play the ghost, Letty. I have delayed long enough. I shall do it tonight, and give Lady Beverly and the rest the fright of their silly lives!"

For once Miss Lorrimer was in complete agreement

with the plan, and eagerly helped with sorting through a quantity of old clothes that had belonged to past generations at Kielder. Soon, silks and satins, shawls, fur tippets, ribbons, lace, and petticoats from bygone days lay higgledy-piggledy about the floor. Near the bottom of the chest they came across a bodice and kirtle of blue brocade, the bodice a tight-fitting, boned affair with a low, square-cut neck, and the kirtle wide and full. Katherine shook out the creases and examined the material carefully.

"It is rather worn, Letty, but that will not matter. I think it will serve very well. It is not precisely right, of course, but the colour and style are similar to the gown in the portrait, and in poor light it will pass. We shall have to contrive a fanshaped ruff somehow, but that should not be too difficult, with all these pieces of lace."

She held the bodice against herself whilst Letty draped the kirtle about her waist. They considered the effect in the looking glass.

"It suits you, Kate. And it will be nice to see you out of mourning, if only for a little while. Black makes you pale."

"Mmm." Katherine studied her reflexion thoughtfully. "I shall have to make some sort of headdress, too. The kind Lady Harriet is wearing. Do you think we could make such a thing?"

Letty, whose skill with a needle was sadly deficient, looked doubtful but willing.

"We can try."

They assembled suitable pieces together and set to work.

"Letty," Miss Spencer mumbled suddenly, several pins in her mouth, "does Cheynings mean anything at all to you? You remember, it was the name of Mr. Drew's country house in the South. Lady Beverly spoke of it."

Miss Lorrimer put down her needle, which instantly unthreaded itself. "Now that you mention it again, Kate, it *does* seem somehow familiar. . . . But I cannot place where I have heard it before. Perhaps it will come to me."

"It's no matter. Could you help me with this ruff? It simply *will* not go right."

By early evening they had finished the costume and hid it in the top of the chest. They shut the lid and looked at each other.

"Suppose you are caught, Kate? The humiliation . . . think of it! They would either be very angry or very amused, and I do not know which would be worse!"

"I shall take good care not to be caught. Don't be fainthearted, Letty. Think how unkind Lady Beverly was to poor Vernon, and what a good lesson this will teach her!"

"Do you mean to teach a lesson to Mr. Drew too? Because I am not sure that he will believe in you."

"With good fortune, I may frighten him as well—for all his scoffing. But it is her ladyship and Mrs. de Vere whom I shall hope to terrify out of their wits!"

As usual, the conversation at the dinner table that evening revolved round Lady Beverly.

"You never dine before half past seven in London, Richard," she began.

"I am not in London at present."

"But dinner at *five o'clock*! Nobody will believe me when I tell them that you have kept such unfashionable hours!"

"Then I should spare yourself the trouble of informing them, Laura," he advised her.

She turned in appeal to Mr. Webber, who, to his intense satisfaction, had been placed next to her.

"*You* do not dine so early, I am certain, Mr. Webber. *You* keep civilised hours at Sudley Hall."

Mr. Webber, who dined even earlier, mumbled vaguely into his soup. The vision his neighbour presented in her white gauze evening gown, a ruby and diamond necklace about her throat, quite overwhelmed him. Mrs. de Vere glittered imposingly, if not so beautifully, in green satin and emeralds opposite him. He looked along the table and observed the contrast between Letitia in her simple puff-sleeved yellow gown and Katherine in her plain black, and the ladies from London, and wondered as he did so whether he had not all along set his sights too low in the selection of his consort. A glorious vision came into his mind of Lady Beverly gracing the foot of his table at Sudley Hall and of himself—elegant and debonair, his cravat tied to perfection—presiding over a gathering of important fashionables. He was awakened from this delightful reverie by Lady Beverly. Turning towards him, she said, "Do tell us more about Sudley Hall, Mr. Webber. I am all *agog* to learn more of it. How many rooms do you have?"

He was thrown into confusion: he had no idea of the answer to this question, and began to add up on his fingers beneath the table. Somewhere on the first floor he lost count and had to begin again. Finally, in desperation, he made a wild guess of thirty.

"Thirty! A mansion indeed," her ladyship exclaimed with a look in Mrs. de Vere's direction. "No wonder you are so proud of your home, Mr. Webber. I daresay *you* have not near that number of rooms in your little house in the country, Richard?"

"I have never counted them," Mr. Drew replied.

Lady Beverly smiled. She plied Mr. Webber with more questions, but if she hoped to render him foolish in describing his home, she was thwarted. He had some reason to be proud of it. Although of no very great size compared with many, Sudley Hall was a fine example of sixteenth-century northern architecture, and he proceeded to inform her of this at some length and in some detail, thereby boring her to death, since she had no real interest whatever in such things, and, although he was quite unaware of it, in doing so, exacting just revenge. Miss Spencer, observing all this, caught Mr. Drew's eye across the table. She wondered how many rooms his little house in the country really did have, and guessed that it was a good many more than Sudley Hall could boast.

After dinner they played whist, but before long Lady Beverly, whose mental powers were severely taxed by this, proposed dancing. Katherine, who danced indifferently and played better, offered herself at the pianoforte. Although she had long since discarded her stick, her ankle still pained her, and provided the perfect excuse.

Will sat beside his sister and watched the dancers in disgust. Since the arrival of the visitors he had been ruthlessly relegated to the background—banished to take meals in the nursery and, worse, to attend to his schoolbooks there under Nurse's eagle eye. He thought dancing silly and viewed the stately change and interchange with glum derision. There was always the hope of a thaw to bring about the party's departure, but it would also bring about the arrival of Mr. Merryman, the vicar, to resume lessons. Will contemplated the unfairness of life. Even shooting had not been so much fun as before, with Lord Beverly missing every bird, blaming the beaters for it, and then losing his temper when he had fallen in a bog and Will had laughed. If he had known what his sister was plotting for the nighttime entertainment of the intruders, he would have cheered up considerably. But Katherine, aware how hard he found it to keep any secret, had told him nothing.

As she played, Miss Spencer also watched the dancers. To Lady Beverly's vexation Mr. Webber had claimed her immediately as a partner, whilst Mr. Drew, whom she had wanted, danced instead with Mrs. de Vere. Mr. Drew danced as elegantly as Katherine had expected, and Mrs. de Vere as haughtily, whilst Lady Beverly, with much affectation and an exaggerated expression of suffering, tried unsuccessfully to avoid her partner's large feet. Letty acquitted herself well, and she and Mr. Lovell made a charming couple.

The dance ended. Lady Beverly hastened to extricate herself from Mr. Webber's eager clasp and fled to Mr. Drew's side. Mrs. de Vere, who knew what her friend expected of her, relinquished her partner and took a turn at the pianoforte. Mr. Lovell, finding himself obliged to surrender Letty to Mr. Webber, came to sit beside Katherine. He complimented her on her playing.

"If I had not met you, Miss Spencer, I should have expected you to disapprove wholeheartedly of such frivolities as music and dancing—not play the pianoforte, as you have just done for us. Harry would have had us believe you quite different, you know."

"So I understand. But I love music, and although I do not dance at all well myself—there is seldom much opportunity for practice at Kielder—there is pleasure to be found in watching others who do. You are all very graceful to behold!"

He smiled wryly. "We have, perhaps, *more* practice than is good for us. Life in London is devoted to such amusements."

"Mr. Drew dances well."

"Who? Oh, Richard. He does everything well. It is excessively annoying."

"You have known him a long time?"

"Since we were born. Our parents are great friends. We were at Eton together. He is insupportably clever, you know, though he likes to give quite the opposite impression."

"It appears that he wastes his talents."

"I suppose he does. His father certainly believes so. Despairs of him . . ." Mr. Lovell cleared his throat. "Wild oats, you know. He'll settle down in the end—we all will." He looked at Letty wistfully.

"Mr. Drew has a sister, as well as a father, I collect."

104

"Did he tell you that? Yes. Louisa's six years younger. Bit of a madcap. She'll be coming out this year. You'd like her. You'd like his mother, too. But she prefers the country—like you. Spends most of her time there. Dotes on Richard."

"I expect she spoiled him as a child."

Mr. Lovell laughed. "Good lord, do you think so? She probably did. Most women do."

"Really?"

"Oh, yes. It must have been a novelty for him to meet you, Miss Spencer. You're the only one I know who doesn't. Everyone in London fawns over him."

"Where does he live, when he is in London," she persisted.

"South Audley Street," he said vaguely. "Near the park."

He turned his head again towards Letty, and Katherine saw that she would get no more information from him.

The ladies retired early, and Mr. Webber, lethargic from grouse and port wine and the heady excitements of the day, followed shortly after. The remaining four gentlemen stayed downstairs to play more hands of whist. Miss Spencer and Miss Lorrimer repaired to effect the transformation of Katherine into Lady Harriet. It took some time, but when they had finished, Letty looked in amazement at the result of their handiwork. In the softness of the candlelight, Katherine looked as though she had stepped down from the portrait in the long gallery. The shortcomings of day had melted away before the night. The headdress that they had cobbled hastily together from bits and pieces looked authentic, and the fan-shaped ruff fashioned from bone and lace convinced entirely. Letty shivered, not only from cold. It was almost too good. Suppose the real Lady Harriet were angered by it all . . . ?

"What are you going to do, Kate?"

"I shall walk along the passage outside Lord and Lady Beverly's chamber, and the de Veres's, and I shall moan like this as I go—" Katherine gave a low, unearthly wail. "Mr. Lovell, fortunately, is on the other side of the castle and so will not be disturbed, Letty."

"Thank heavens."

"And Will and Nurse sleep on the floor above and will hear nothing."

"What about Vernon?"

"Good God, Vernon! I had forgotten him! He is only two rooms away from the Beverlys. But he is bound to sleep soundly as a babe."

There was a scratching sound at the door, and Letty, whose nerves were in tatters, gave a small shriek.

"It's only Boots."

Miss Spencer opened the door and the spaniel padded in wearing an air of injured dignity. His fireside could no longer be called his own: his tail had been trodden on three times in the past half hour. He walked to the fireplace in the bedchamber and lay down in front of an altogether inferior blaze.

"Poor Boots," said Katherine. "If he were not such a good-natured animal, he would bite Lord Beverly's ankle!"

Through the open door came the sound of male laughter from below.

"How much longer are they going to stay down there?" Letty wondered in despair.

They tiptoed to the galleried landing and peered down over the balustrade into the great hall. The whist game had finished and the gentlemen were gathered round the fire, Lord Beverly, as usual, commandeering the hearth. Mr. Drew leaned against the chimneypiece, whilst Mr. Lovell sat with legs outstretched, and—astonishing spectacle—Mr. de Vere could be seen wide awake and talking, if not with animation, at least spasmodically. All four held glasses that from the look of things would seem to have been refilled many times. There was another burst of loud laughter.

"They're drunk!" Letty whispered, dismayed.

"So much the better. They will believe what they see all the more readily."

"If they do not fall either asleep or over first."

The prospect, admittedly, was not promising: the gentlemen showed no sign of disbanding and every sign of remaining. Miss Spencer and Miss Lorrimer retreated and settled down, in company with Boots, to wait. One hour passed and then another, before at last the rumbling and stumbling of voices and footsteps could be heard coming upstairs. Letty had loyally remained at her post but fallen sound asleep in the chair, and Katherine saw no reason to disturb her. She opened the door quietly and set off, candle in hand, through the darkness of the castle.

She had formed a plan of starting from the south tower and making her way gradually northwards, so that the moaning would be heard very faintly at first, echoing eerily as she progressed through the castle. Her long skirts swept the ground as she walked and dulled the sound of her feet; she held the fluttering candle beneath her chin to give the ghostliest effect.

A pattering sound behind her made her blood freeze and her heart race. She turned, but could see nothing at first, until two green eyes shone suddenly in the candle-light.

"Boots! Go back at once! You are *not* to follow me, do you hear?"

The spaniel wagged his tail and blinked hopefully.

"You disobedient dog," Katherine told him, despairingly. "Why do you never do anything I tell you, and why was I so stupid as to leave the door open!"

Boots looked guilty but stood his ground.

"Go back, you bad boy! Do as I say this minute."

The spaniel's eyes drooped.

There was little hope of him returning to her room, but some that he might not follow her too closely. With further admonitions, Katherine left him sitting there and continued on her way.

Her plan, at first, worked better than she had dared expect. As she neared the north tower, emitting low wails, Mrs. de Vere emerged from her room, holding a candle before her. On perceiving Lady Harriet, she uttered a loud shriek and stood as though turned to stone. Her husband had evidently already fallen into a deep slumber, for he did not rush to his lady's aid, and the task fell instead to Lord Beverly, who stuck his nightcapped head out from the adjoining room.

"What in thunder . . . ?"

Mrs. de Vere pointed wordlessly and with a shaking hand to a spot behind him. Lord Beverly turned and gaped. Lady Beverly, doll-like in her white lawn nightrobe, then appeared in the doorway. To Miss Spencer's immense satisfaction she screamed even louder than Mrs. de Vere and looked ready to faint.

Katherine passed them by and, moaning faintly, floated on down the dark passageway towards the north tower. As she did so, Mr. Webber came forth from his bedchamber and goggled soundlessly at the apparition that met his gaze. He looked so absurd in his nightshirt, with bare feet, that Katherine almost gave a laugh but managed to turn it into a sobbing cry.

Mrs. de Vere found her voice. "It's a ghost! It's Lady Harriet! Oh, my God, I am going to faint!"

She did not, however, but rushed to Lord Beverly's side and seized hold of his left arm, whilst Lady Beverly clutched his right; they clung tightly to him.

His lordship staggered a little. "Ghosht, be damned!" he cried. "Don't believe in 'em! Some funny bishness! Some damned trick! I'm going to find out!"

He snatched the candle from Mrs. de Vere's nerveless

fingers, shook off both ladies as mercilessly as if they had been newborn kittens, and lurched off in pursuit of the disappearing figure.

Miss Spencer, hearing what sounded like a maddened bull behind her, increased her pace. If she could reach the door to the north tower she would be safe, for she knew all the twists and turns of the stairway and passages far too well to be caught there. Her long skirts hindered her, however, and she nearly tripped and fell. She picked up the kirtle and began to run—although a ghost would surely never have done so—fleeing before her pursuer. As she went, the candle blew out, leaving her in perilous darkness. The ignominy of capture seemed certain, when she heard the sound of barking, followed by violent curses from Lord Beverly. Boots had come to her rescue! She paused, panting hard, and then turned for the door to the north tower and safety.

"Good evening, Lady Harriet!"

The mocking voice sounded from the darkness. Not knowing what to say, she wisely said nothing. She could hear Boots growling ferociously and Lord Beverly shouting furiously. A loud yelp from the spaniel warned her that his lordship had gained the upper hand and, freed of another encumbrance, was certainly advancing towards her.

"Mr. Drew . . ."

It was a supplication. Before she could say more, she felt herself grasped none too gently and thrust forward into blackness. She fell to her knees, for a moment too stunned to move. Then, feeling about her, she realised that she was in the old broom cupboard near the entrance to the north tower. She could hear the irate tones of Lord Beverly on the other side of the door.

"Confound it, I tell you I saw it come this way. Some female dressed up as that Harriet woman, or whatever she's called. If it hadn't been for that damned dog, I'd have caught her."

Mr. Drew answered him. "I saw nobody, George. Are you sure you weren't having a nightmare?"

"Great God, we all three saw it—and that Webber fellow too. Saw it as clear as I'm shtanding here. . . . Something familiar about her, though I'm bleshed if I can think—"

"Perhaps the brandy did not agree with you."

There was an indulgent denial. "Don't know what you mean, Melvin. I'm as sober as you—which ain't saying much. I know what I saw, and it wasn't some damned ghost. It was flesh and blood. I'll shtake my life on it!"

Katherine moved closer to the door to hear better, and something shifted beside her and fell with a clatter.

"What was that?"

"What was what?"

"That noise . . . it came from that door behind you. Out of my way—"

There was a thud against the cupboard door, and the sound of a scuffle. Miss Spencer recoiled in the darkness.

"I must insist that you leave it to me, Beverly," Mr. Drew's voice did not encourage argument. "It was probably one of the servants playing a trick, and I shall make the necessary enquiries in the morning. Meanwhile, I suggest you go back to bed and tell the others to do the same. It's far too cold to stand about here."

This was uncomfortably true. Lord Beverly grunted, demurred, and finally consented, though with poor grace. His heavy and resentful tread could be heard going away down the passage. Katherine did not dare to move. She waited, listening, and then heard the key turn in the lock. Then there was silence again. She tried the door. It was locked.

There was no need to panic, she told herself. Some-one—and it could only be Mr. Drew—had shut her in deliberately for a joke. She had only to wait, and sooner or later he would come and release her. She waited. Time passed—she had no idea how long—and with each passing minute she felt more frightened and more indignant. The cupboard was small, pitch black, and crowded with all kinds of cleaning implements. She felt about her, and her fingers encountered the woolly head of a mop; she found herself clutching it to her for comfort in an absurd fashion. Whatever happened, she must stay calm. Much as she longed to pound and shout at the door, she must not give Mr. Drew the satisfaction of seeing how thoroughly he had alarmed her. He was drunk, and therefore capable of anything, but surely he would not leave her here all night! Letty would miss her, but Letty was probably still fast asleep, and in any case would be much too terrified to come out in search of her. More time passed. Katherine began to despair, and sank to the floor in a despondent heap.

A moment later there was the sound of footsteps outside, and she raised her head in hope. The handle rattled loudly and the door shook. She heard Lord Beverly muttering and cursing, and for the first time had cause to be thankful that the door was locked. After a few minutes, he gave up and went away, and there was silence again. More time passed, and despite the cold, Katherine began to doze, the mop cradled in her arms. She was startled into wakefulness by the sound of the key turning once more. The door opened and she blinked into candlelight.

Mr. Drew stepped into the cupboard and pulled the door shut behind him. Katherine had never imagined that the moment would come when she would be glad to see him—so glad that if her cramped limbs had allowed it she might easily have jumped up into his arms. That feeling, however, was short-lived. She saw the expression on his face, lit eerily from below by the candle he held, and quailed in her corner. For the first time, she felt at fault with him, and in consequence felt also for the first time, if not precisely afraid, at least apprehensive. He had every right to be vexed with her, there was no denying it. The deception which had started with such confidence and zeal now appeared rather foolish and even despicable. Her costume, with its low-cut bodice and home-sewn trimmings, seemed vulgar, and her whole situation humiliating and ridiculous. She clasped the mop to her and was silent.

Mr. Drew jerked her roughly and without ceremony to her feet. There was barely room for one, let alone two, in the cupboard, and Katherine found herself pressed uncomfortably against him. Miss Lorrimer would undoubtedly have admired the splendour of his embroidered dressing gown and noted how well it became him, but Miss Spencer in her confusion saw none of this.

"I seem to remember that we had agreed a truce, you and I, or had you forgotten?" he said unpleasantly. "What exactly did you hope to achieve with this latest piece of nonsense?" His fingers flicked at the lace on her bodice. "This suits you very well, but surely you didn't expect it to deceive me?"

"I only meant to frighten Lady Beverly and Mrs. de Vere—"

"Then you succeeded. Unfortunately, you quite failed to convince his lordship. If you had consulted me before, I could have told you that he would never believe in any ghost. Beverly has no imagination—drunk or sober. I really should have let him catch you, Miss Spencer. You deserved it."

"I'm grateful to you," she said sullenly.

"I don't believe a word of it. You look as though you are about to hit me with that mop."

"There was no need to lock me in here for so long."

"I recollect that you had no compunction in doing the same to me, once. If I hadn't locked the door, Beverly would have discovered you. Besides, I had a mind to teach you a lesson." He rested the flat of his hand against the wall behind her head. She turned her face from his.

"You reek of brandy!"

"And you of camphor from that old dress. We make a fine pair, don't you agree?"

She felt as though she might suffocate in that small space, but there was no escape: he stood between her and the door.

"Will you let me go . . . please!"

"That's unaccustomed politeness from you, Kate."

"I shall faint!"

"No, you won't. You are not the fainting kind." He looked down at her, unsmiling. "I'm very tired of your tricks, you see. I'm very tired of your games. In fact, I have quite lost patience with you, Miss Spencer. And I shall not let you out of this cupboard until you have given me your promise that you will cease all these absurd hostilities forthwith."

Katherine felt that she really might faint if she had to stay there much longer; or if she did not faint, she would begin to scream or cry or beg, and very possibly all three. Capitulation was the only dignified course.

"Very well," she muttered ungraciously. "I promise."

"Upon your honour?"

"Upon my honour. And *now* will you please let me go?"

He made no move to free her. Instead he leaned still closer. "If we are no longer to be sworn enemies, Kate, then we must surely be friends. The bargain should be properly sealed."

She brought the mop between them. "You have not yet kept your side of it, Mr. Drew. You said you would release me."

"And you are already forgetting yours. I said *all* hostilities, Miss Spencer. You are planning to hit me with that mop. You must show more goodwill than that." He set the candlestick on the high shelf above her head. "It would be a pity for that magnificent gown to suffer the same fate as my cravat."

He was smiling as he spoke, his anger apparently

113

gone, but Katherine was in no way reassured. She looked away, but he took her chin in his hand and turned her back towards him. Since she could neither advance nor retreat, her only defence was to lift the mop in front of her face like a shield.

Mr. Drew pushed the mop firmly to one side. Katherine tried to duck, but as he still held her chin this did not succeed either.

"If you will not show goodwill, Kate, then I must."

His face was now in shadow, but if she could not see his expression, his intention was very clear. There being nothing left to do, Katherine shut her eyes.

The first time he had kissed her had been a brief and insulting experience. This was different. It was still insulting, but it was certainly not brief, nor was it a mere token to seal a bargain. Miss Spencer found herself crushed against the cupboard wall in a kiss that petrified her senses: she could not move, think, speak, or even breathe. It was beyond anything she had ever imagined. Her headdress went awry, her gown slid from one shoulder, and by the time he finally let her go, both her ruff collar and her self-possession had collapsed.

"That was unnecessary," she said bitterly, when she had found her voice. "How dare you!"

"The longer the kiss the stronger the bargain," he replied, taking the candlestick down from the shelf. "Your lace has slipped, by the way. Permit me to help you."

"No, thank you."

She tried to repair the damage with fingers that shook as though with ague. The headdress was past mending and the big ruff collar had flopped about her shoulders. The rest she rearranged as best she could.

"*Now* may I go?"

"Certainly."

He opened the door and stepped out, holding it open

for her. "You're lucky, Kate. Women don't usually escape from me in such circumstances."

With freedom from that confined space some of Katherine's old jauntiness returned. "I imagine they always fall at your feet in any case, Mr. Drew, and save you the trouble of detaining them."

"They do. But that can be tedious. I prefer at least some pretence at resistance."

"*I* was not pretending, if that is what you imagine."

"I know."

She looked about her. "My candle. It must still be in the cupboard."

"I will fetch it."

He reentered the cupboard, and as he did so Katherine had the wild idea of slamming the door shut and locking him in. A fit and just punishment, she considered, for the humiliation he had inflicted on her. She had moved a step forward and had her hand on the doorknob when he emerged.

"That would have served little purpose, Miss Spencer. I have the key in my pocket. Did you think I trusted you? I have your candle here."

Katherine waited in silence while he lit her candle from his own. The two flames illuminated his face brightly. Her gaze rested on his mouth. It was a nice mouth, she had to admit—strong, and with humourous curves at the corners. She stared, remembering.

He looked up from the candle, and seeing her stare, smiled.

She said stiffly, "Are you going to tell them the truth?"

"The truth?"

"About—about the ghost."

"Not so long as you keep your promise. It will be far more entertaining to leave them wondering. Beverly will suspect every maidservant in the castle, whilst the others will believe they really saw a ghost." He held out her candle to her. "Isn't that what you wanted? Take this and fly, your ladyship. Vanish into the night like all well-behaved ghosts! I have shut your badly behaved gun dog in my room, by the by. Beverly might have suspected you were in the cupboard, but Boots would have known you were and given you away." He bowed. "Good night, Lady Harriet."

She swept him a low and equally ironic curtsey.

"Good night . . . Mr. Drew."

It was several days before Lord Beverly relinquished his search for the ghost or its perpetrator. He roamed about the castle, poking in every corner and staring hard and suspiciously at all the servants. The cupboard, when opened to satisfy him, proved to his annoyance to contain nothing more than mops and dusters and brooms, and although he remained unsatisfied and kept vigil for three nights, he discovered nothing that might have led him to the truth. Lady Beverly and Mrs. de Vere, though recovered from their initial fright, were still much chastened by the experience and plainly believed in Lady Harriet. Mr. Lovell, who had slept sound as a babe, laughed loudly at the mere idea, but Mr. Webber, after some sober pondering and reflexion, began to suspect the identity of the ghost. He said nothing, but considered that if he were right, he had done well to withdraw his suit. Such behaviour was unthinkable and, coupled with the episode of the dungeon, merited severe censure. He was also gravely disappointed in Letitia, who had lately had eyes for no one but Mr. Lovell—a younger son, so he understood, without any fortune to his name, let alone the advantage of a residence comparable with Sudley Hall.

When the thaw came it was a relief to nearly everyone at Kielder, and immediate plans were made for the London party to depart forthwith. Lady Beverly declared herself never more thankful to quit any place on earth—a sentiment dutifully echoed, as usual, by Mrs. de Vere. Mr. Lovell, alone of them, was reluctant to leave.

"Damn it, Richard," he said to his friend in private, "how can I leave? And yet how can I stay?"

"You are talking in riddles, David."

"You know very well what I mean. What a cold fish you are! What am I to do about Miss Lorrimer?"

"Marry her, if she will have you, and if that is what you want."

"I told you—I won't be thought a fortune hunter."

"So you did. But why should you be?"

"Confound it, I've only known her ten days—ten days and six hours, to be precise. What else would anyone think but that I am after her fortune?"

"Some might think that you had fallen in love with Miss Lorrimer straightaway, rather than taking your time about it," Mr. Drew observed.

"Don't joke about it, Richard. I am in deadly earnest."

"Then tell her so. Assuredly she is only waiting for you to do so."

Mr. Lovell brightened. "Do you think so? Do you *really* think so? Is she not adorable!"

"Enchanting."

Mr. Lovell relapsed suddenly into gloom. "But I cannot address her yet. . . . It is too soon. It would not be right. I shall go back to London. She will forget me."

"Unlikely, I think, but always possible. You're a fool, David, but I can see you will not listen to me. You are quite determined on your course." He took a delicate pinch of snuff. "Incidentally, I shall be returning with you myself now—for a few days, at least. I received an urgent summons from my father this morning, couched in no uncertain terms. It seems he requires my signature for various documents. Tedious, but necessary."

"You have not told him—"

"Is that likely? He thinks I am staying here with

friends. You may rest easy, David. His wrath would not, in any case, descend on *your* head."

"Thank God for that!" Mr. Lovell shivered. "I don't mind telling you that I find your papa a shade daunting."

"When he is angry, it is usually with good reason."

"And you have given him plenty of good reasons!"

"He was quite as badly behaved in his own youth, and his father before him. And his father's father. I come from a very long line of rakes, who all turn martinet once they become parents."

"Well, if you are returning to London and leaving Kielder, you have lost fifty guineas!" Mr. Lovell held out his hand.

"Ah, but there was no stipulation that I should stay here the whole time, if you remember. And I shall be back before the end of the month."

"An unfair advantage!"

"Not at all. I gave *you* an unfair advantage in inviting you here—not to mention having the Beverlys and the de Veres, who nearly gave me away several times."

"True. I thought for a while that Miss Spencer suspected. It was lucky for you that she had never heard of Cheynings. Anyway, thirty guineas will certainly come my way. I should have made it a hundred on such a certainty!"

The news that Mr. Drew was to leave with the rest of the party raised Miss Spencer's hopes that he might finally have tired of Kielder, but these were quickly dashed by the information that he was to return later. The memory of the broom cupboard still lingered, and she had avoided being alone with him ever since.

He took his leave of her with his customary irony.

"I know you will bear my absence with fortitude."

"I shall endeavour not to sink into a decline without you, Mr. Drew."

"Console yourself that I shall be back before the end of the month."

"That thought will support me through the dark days."

He smiled, and then said seriously, "There is one other matter. If Harry left any bills unpaid in London, I should be happy to discharge them for you whilst I am there. You can repay me whenever you wish."

She stared at him. "There are no bills, Mr. Drew."

He shrugged as though it were of no concern to him. "As you please." He took her hand in his and kissed it lightly in farewell.

When they had gone, Katherine thought that Kielder had never seemed so quiet. Her spirits, which should have been high at the resumption of this peace, were unaccountably low. Even Mr. Webber's departure failed to lift them. And poor Letty was inconsolable.

"I shall never see Mr. Lovell again, Kate! I shall die of a broken heart! Or throw myself off the battlements!"

"You would only fall in the moat."

"Then I should drown. For I can't swim a stroke, you know. I should drown with grief like Ophelia and float along 'larded with sweet flowers.' "

"Ophelia had long hair, not cut à la Titus. And it's winter, so there aren't any flowers. Oh, Letty, don't despair. I'm sure he will come back. I know he loves you—anyone can see that. How could he not! I expect he felt it too soon to declare himself."

Letty shook her head sadly. "It's more than that. I think it is because of my Connexion with Trade. His family is very old and grand, you see. I daresay they would not approve at all."

"I cannot believe that Mr. Lovell would care two pins about that. There must be some other reason."

"I'm afraid there is not."

Miss Spencer had been absently stroking Boots's ears; she was silent for a moment, and then said suddenly, "I may be able to help you, Letty."

"I wish you could, but I don't see how."

"You see, I have made up my mind about something. I am going to London."

"Kate! Have you gone mad! What for? You have always sworn you would never go within a hundred miles of the place."

Katherine drew a deep breath. "I am going to London, nonetheless. Because I am going to find out the truth about Mr. Drew."

"The truth about him? What do you mean?"

"I told you that there is some mystery about him. I have suspected it for a long time, and now I am sure of it—ever since the night I dressed up as Lady Harriet."

"And I must say I thought it very generous of Mr. Drew not to give you away, Kate. If I were him, I think I should have been quite angry."

"It amused him too much." Katherine smiled at the memory. "You should have seen Vernon's face, Letty! His eyes nearly popped out of his head! And Lord Beverly was just like an angry bull!"

"Then I am very glad he did not catch you—and *that* was only due to Mr. Drew."

"The point is, Letty, that when I was in the cupboard I could hear every word that Lord Beverly said to Mr. Drew. And he addressed him as *Melvin*. What do you think of that?"

"That Mr. Drew has two names and is called Richard Melvin Drew. I myself am Letitia Mary, and my mother was always called by her second name, Elaine. There is nothing very mysterious about that."

"Yes, there is. I am certain of it. Mr. Drew may not be Mr. Drew at all, in which case—don't you see, Letty—Kielder does not belong to him, after all."

Miss Lorrimer looked slightly bewildered. "So, what will you do when you are in London, Kate?"

"Mr. Lovell told me that Mr. Drew lives in South Audley Street, near the park. I propose to go and see for myself whether he does live there, and whether he is who he pretends to be. At the same time, I shall probably meet Mr. Lovell, as he is such a close friend of Mr. Drew's, and will be able to establish if what you believe is really true."

Letty considered this for a moment. As she did so, another idea came to her, a very simple and delightful notion that brought a flush of excitement to her cheeks and a sparkle to her eyes. The air of dejection was gone.

"If you are going to London, Kate," she said, "then I am coming too!"

=8=

WHEN MR. LORRIMER learned that Katherine would accompany his daughter, he reluctantly gave his consent to the proposed trip to London. It was arranged that they would stay with Mrs. Jennings, Letty's aunt in Kensington, Mr. Lorrimer having expressed the opinion that the good sense of Miss Spencer would fortunately counterbalance the nonsense of his sister-in-law—not to mention that of his daughter. He gave the expedition his sanction, if not precisely his approval, and, furthermore, insisted on bearing the greater part of the cost of hiring a post chaise-and-four. Katherine protested at this generosity, but he merely said that he was indebted to her, rather than the reverse. She could only be grateful for his kindness; to travel otherwise would have necessitated enduring all the discomforts and miseries of the stage, with the dangers and tribulations of drunken coachmen, freezing cold, and bug-ridden inns.

As it was, a journey with only herself, Letty, and Letty's maid, even by hired post chaise, could not be described as anything other than tiring and tedious. The excitement of departure soon wore off, and even Letty's enjoyment faded as they proceeded slowly south. York, Newark, Grantham, and Stamford were reached and then left behind.

"But every mile is a mile nearer London," Miss Lorrimer said, as much to cheer herself as anyone else. "And it is all so very *different* from the North."

Katherine, watching the passing scenery, had formed the same conclusion. The further south they travelled, the more alien their surroundings: the rugged wildness of her native county had been replaced by flat, featureless land that stretched drearily into the far distance, and the few trees to be seen were bent and bowed by the wind. So far she had not seen any justification for Lady Beverly's scorn of the North.

It took five days to reach London, and when their post chaise finally came within sight and sound of the great city, they were almost too stiff and exhausted to take much note. But as they drove through the streets, the colour, the noise, and the teeming life about them made them forget their tiredness and stare in amazement.

"*London!*" breathed Letty, her nose pressed against the window. "London! At *last!*"

Mrs. Jennings lived in a tall white house in Kensington, a pleasant village on the south side of the city. A widow of comfortable means and without any children of her own, she lived alone, but what might otherwise have been a dull life was enlivened by her insatiable interest in Society. She studied the *Gazette* rigourously, noting every item of news, however small or trivial. There was little she did not know about official happenings amongst the *haut ton*, and thanks to her excellent sources, not much either that she did not know about the unofficial happenings. Her curiosity about the affairs of others did not stem so much from a vulgar tendency to poke and pry as from the lack of a family of her own. Other people's children and their alliances were meat and drink to her. Titles she adored, and could recite a list of all the premier families in the land, as well as tales about each one. She favoured bright colours, and her house made visitors blink before their eyes adjusted to the glare of scarlet aligned with magenta and saffron yellow married to emerald green. She dressed colourfully herself, despite her widowhood, and in a style rather too young for her age, while her hair owed nothing to nature and was frizzed in girlish curls over her ears. Miss Spencer, after a short acquaintance, thought she saw why Mr. Lorrimer, with his dour, northern ethos, should consider Mrs. Jennings a somewhat unsuitable mentor for his beloved daughter. But beneath the frills and fripperies and the endless stream of gossiping chatter there lay a warm heart and a good deal of shrewdness.

Letty, watching the fashionables from the front window, bemoaned, as usual, the dowdiness of her own gowns. Her aunt, however, surprisingly disagreed.

"They may not be in the very forefront of fashion, it is true, but whatever you wear will look charming because *you* are charming, my dear. We may do a *little* shopping, of course, but nothing too extravagant, or your dear papa will disapprove. Besides, the Season has not yet nearly begun and there is hardly anyone in town."

Remembering the crowded pavements they had passed, Katherine thought this remark rather amusing, but she kept a straight face and listened politely to Mrs. Jennings's account of her recent visit to Brighton. Mention of that seaside town to which Harry had raced to his death reminded her also of the object of her journey, and she decided to waste no time in pursuing it. She had quickly realised that the widow was the very person to help her, and, accordingly, when Mrs. Jennings paused for breath after a long description of the Pavilion, which she had much admired, Katherine enquired if she knew anything of a Mr. Drew of South Audley Street.

Mrs. Jennings frowned. This was a rare gap in her knowledge. "Mr. Drew . . . let me see . . . I don't think . . . Do you know, I cannot for the moment recall any gentleman of that name. Is he of consequence, my dear?"

"I believe so."

"South Audley Street is certainly an excellent address. Drew . . . Drew." Finally, the widow shook her head. "I am sorry to say that I do not know of any Mr. Drew. He certainly is not in the first rank of Society, or else I should have heard of him." She darted Katherine a bright and penetrating look. "These young gentlemen sometimes like to give themselves consequence that they do not, in reality, possess, to impress ladies. Your Mr. Drew is probably a complete nobody. In which case, it is as well to have discovered it."

Miss Spencer said nothing. Mrs. Jennings was not infallible, but the only way to find out the truth about Mr. Drew seemed to be to go to South Audley Street, as she had originally planned. And this she now proposed to do at the very first opportunity.

Letty, emboldened by Katherine's enquiry, followed with one of her own, after Mr. Lovell, and met with far more success. Her aunt pounced upon the name.

"Lovell! Oh, yes, indeed. An old family, from Hertfordshire, I fancy. Sir John must be the eighth baronet at least. He married Minnie Wingfield, and *she* was a great beauty in her day. They had . . . let me think a moment . . . four sons and one—or it might have been two—daughters. Mr. *David* Lovell did you say? Now, he would be the second or third son—I cannot quite recall which, but it will be a simple matter to look it up in a moment." She patted her niece's hand. "A very *good* family, my dear, but if I remember correctly, the previous baronet made some rather unwise investments and reduced the family circumstances somewhat. If I were you I should always pay more attention to the eldest son. Younger sons are so *awkwardly* placed. Are you well acquainted with Mr. Lovell?"

Letty explained, blushing a little, and added that he was a close friend of Mr. Drew, and that both gentlemen were presently in town. Mrs. Jennings looked puzzled.

"It is all the odder, then, that I have not heard of this other gentleman, since they must both move in the same circles. However, doubtless there is some simple explanation." She smiled indulgently at her niece. "You will be anxious to renew your acquaintanceship with Mr. Lovell while you are in London. Do not worry, my dear. With a little ingenuity I am sure I can manage to arrange it. I have a very good friend, Lady Mablethorpe, who frequently gives evening parties—just small gatherings, you know, with perhaps a little music and cards; nothing out of the way, but most enjoyable. It would be an easy matter to prevail upon her to invite Mr. Lovell."

Letty was transported with delight—and then just as quickly cast down again by the thought that she had nothing fit to wear for such an occasion. After some discussion on the subject, Mrs. Jennings gave way to her pleas, and a shopping expedition was proposed for the following day. The widow was very fond of shopping and, despite the long-reaching shadow of her brother-in-law's disapproval, soon fell to planning a wardrobe for her niece. Miss Spencer, listening, was doubtful of the advice her friend was receiving, but seeing she could do nothing, went to look out of the window and watch the passing traffic of carriages and carts. After Kielder, she still could not accustom herself to such noise and activity. She looked and listened and wondered where in the great city Mr. Drew was to be found at that moment.

On the following morning Mrs. Jennings and Letty set off for the shops. Katherine had been invited to accompany them but pleaded fatigue. However, soon after they had left the house, she herself followed, but on foot, and in what she hoped was the direction of South Audley Street.

Having no knowledge of London proved a grave handicap. She was misdirected several times, lost her way countless others, and all but gave up in despair. She might have saved herself a great deal of trouble by hiring a hackney, but she did not even know of such a thing. The narrow streets were not only crowded with all manner of vehicles—private carriages, coaches, overladen drays and carts—but were also shockingly dirty. As she made her way through London she was jostled and pushed on every side, assailed by appalling smells, and horrified by the ugliness and poverty that she witnessed. At one time she was almost run down by a herd of cattle being driven to slaughter, and the sight of one animal making a futile dash for freedom only to be cornered, with heaving flanks and terrified eyes, against a wall, filled her with revulsion and helpless pity.

When she finally reached South Audley Street she was tired, dishevelled and disillusioned. The quiet elegance of the street with its long line of gracious houses seemed an unbelievable contrast to everything she had previously experienced. Here was wealth. Here was prosperity. Here was Society.

She began, bravely, at the first house. The door was opened by an imposing manservant, who surveyed her from an unbending height. His cold stare took in the untidiness of her dress and the mud on her petticoat. No, he informed her, there was no Mr. Drew resident there. There had never been such a gentleman, and, it was implied, it was most unlikely that there ever would be anyone with so undistinguished and ordinary a name residing at that house. From this Katherine deduced that the house was occupied by a duke, at the very least.

The door knocker had been removed from the next house, indicating that its owner was out of town. The one after proved equally unfruitful, and at the house after that she was viewed with deep suspicion and directed to the servants' entrance. A long row of doors still stretched before her, and it required a stern reminder to herself of what was at stake before Katherine felt able to continue.

At the tenth house, the black-painted door was opened by a liveried footman. When, in answer to his enquiry, she asked for Mr. Drew, he looked at first surprised and then disconcerted.

"You wish to see Mr. Drew?"

Miss Spencer's heart missed a beat. "If you please."

The young man hesitated, and then, having examined her more carefully, made up his mind. He held the door open wider and allowed her to step into the hall.

Katherine found herself in the most sumptuous and impressive surroundings. To one accustomed to austerity and shabbiness, the richness and opulence was awesome. She waited, admiring—if not actually liking—an immense marble-topped table on which reposed a large porcelain candelabrum with ormolu mounts. She would have liked to sit down on one of the magnificent gilt chairs, since her legs were exceedingly tired and rather shaky with nervousness, but she did not dare. Now that she was actually in Mr. Drew's house, the prospect of coming face to face with him and explaining her presence was alarming. It was evident that he had not deceived her after all, and that he was a great deal richer and more important than she had ever imagined.

After a few moments the young footman returned with another manservant—a butler, who advanced towards Miss Spencer with stately and measured tread.

"I understand you wish to see me, madam."

Obviously she had not made herself sufficiently clear. "It is Mr. Drew I wish to see."

The butler regarded her gravely. One glance, at more than twenty paces, had been sufficient for his unerring and practised eye to see that, despite her appearance, the visitor was a gentlewoman and one of considerable refinement. He bowed.

"*I* am Mr. Drew, ma'am. Pray, how may I serve you?"

"*You* are Mr. Drew?"

"That is my name. I am butler to his lordship."

"His lordship?" Miss Spencer repeated stupidly.

"The Earl of Ingram. This is his lordship's residence."

It was clear that she had made an embarrassing and silly mistake: the coincidence of the butler having the same name was most unfortunate. Blushing and stammering, Katherine began to make her apologies and to retreat as she did so towards the front door. To explain satisfactorily was well-nigh impossible, and all she could do was to murmur that she had been mistaken on account of her poor knowledge of London. She reached the door anxious to escape as quickly as possible.

"What is it, Drew?"

A gentleman was descending the sweeping staircase at the far end of the hall; he moved unhurriedly, one hand resting lightly on the bannister.

The butler turned towards his master deferentially. "It is nothing, my lord. This young lady mistook this house for another, being a stranger to London."

"I see."

The earl paused at the foot of the staircase and raised his eyeglass to examine Miss Spencer. He was a tall man, well past middle age but still extremely handsome. He was exquisitely dressed, and his manner and speech could only bespeak breeding and privilege. Even if she had not already known him to be an earl, Katherine felt she would have guessed him to be a nobleman. With the utmost civility, and as though there were nothing unusual in finding a strange female invading his house on the flimsiest pretext, he asked her name.

Miss Spencer curtsied and told him, adding still more apologies for the trouble she had caused.

He smiled politely, although the smile did not reach his eyes. "Please do not concern yourself, Miss Spencer. It is very easy to lose oneself in London, if one is not well acquainted with the city. We must do what we can to help you. Have you a carriage waiting?"

"No, sir. I—I walked."

She was miserably aware of how she must appear to the earl, with her crumpled gown and her mud-stained petticoats, not realising that her very dishevelment lent credence to her story. She looked the picture of a lady in distress.

The earl stroked his chin thoughtfully. "From where did you walk, Miss Spencer?"

"From Kensington."

"Kensington!"

He spoke as though she had mentioned some distant, foreign country. It had not occurred to Katherine before that there was anything unusual in walking such a distance in London; she was used to walking a good deal farther at home.

"You must be tired and in need of rest and refreshment," the earl went on. "My wife is in the country at present, but I trust you will allow me to take her place and offer you both."

His command to his butler was no more than the slightest movement of his left hand, but the man interpreted this instantly and, bowing, removed himself. Miss Spencer was then conducted into a small saloon, which was beautifully furnished. The walls were hung with rose damask set in white moulded panels, and the curtains of gold silk were very long, and draped so that their heavy folds swept the carpet as elegantly as a woman's gown. There were two settees, some fine walnut chairs, and a tall walnut bureau. The chimneypiece was of marble and decorated with pilasters and a frieze of urns entwined with garlands. A fire burned brightly in the polished steel grate. Mrs. Jennings would have liked it exceedingly, Katherine thought, except that she might have considered the colours rather too muted for her taste.

Small cakes and lemonade were brought, and she accepted them gratefully, as she was both hungry and thirsty. The earl remained standing beside the fire and waited a while before speaking again.

"May I ask, Miss Spencer, whom you were seeking

when you came to my house in error? I may be able to direct you there. I know a great many people in London."

She felt herself colouring. "It is most kind of you, my lord, but I do not think that you will be able to help me."

"Be sensible, Miss Spencer. You wish to find someone. I may be able to put you on the right path. I shall not, I assure you, pry into your private affairs."

She hesitated. "The circumstances are somewhat . . . somewhat unusual."

"So I deduce."

"In fact, they are quite *odd*."

"Tell me."

She looked up at him. He had very cold blue eyes, and she felt that he was not a man she would care to cross. He was hard, she thought, but probably a just person, and someone to be trusted and relied upon completely. It was unlikely that he would be deceived were she to tell him less than the whole truth.

"I am looking for a Mr. Drew," she said.

He raised an eyebrow. "Not my butler, I collect?"

"No, my lord. That is where the confusion arose. When I asked to see Mr. Drew, it was thought, of course, that I wished to see him."

"I cannot conceive how they could have imagined you likely to have any dealings with the butler," he remarked. "But we will pass over that." He drew a small enamel box from his waistcoat pocket and, using his right hand alone, flicked open the lid with his thumbnail and took a pinch of snuff. Something about this struck a chord in Miss Spencer's mind which she could not place. "You are acquainted with this elusive Mr. Drew, I take it? You are not in search of some gentleman unknown to yourself?"

"I am indeed acquainted with him."

"An acquaintanceship which, to judge from your tone, does not seem to have brought you much pleasure," the earl observed drily. "And yet you walk from *Kensington* in search of him."

"I have reason to believe that he may not be precisely what he pretended to be."

"Dear me, how very complicated. No wonder your search is so difficult." The earl seated himself opposite her and rested his cheek on his hand. A heavy gold signet gleamed on his little finger. "Tell me, at least, what or who he pretends to be."

"A gentleman of that name living in South Audley Street."

"You are quite sure it was South Audley Street?"

"Yes, I am sure. Near the park. We are near the park, are we not?"

"We are indeed. But I can tell you one thing for certain, Miss Spencer: there is no Mr. Drew—apart from my butler—residing in South Audley Street. No gentleman of that name. I take it that he *is* a gentleman?"

"Oh, yes."

"Then I am very much afraid you were either mistaken or have been misled—deliberately or otherwise. Is there nothing else you know of this Mr. Drew which might help us find him for you?"

"He has a country house, I believe, but of course you would not know it, sir."

"I have a country house myself, and I might well know it."

"It is called Cheynings."

The earl moved in his chair and leaned his cheek on his other hand. "You do intrigue me, Miss Spencer. I should like to hear more about Mr. Drew. Tell me, was he young or old? Tall or short? Fat or thin? Dark or fair? Ugly or handsome?"

Katherine considered all this. "He is tall—about your height, I should say, my lord, and fair . . . young, and remarkably handsome—which he knows very well."

"Charming?"

"Very—when he wishes to be."

"And I have no doubt that he would wish to be to you, Miss Spencer. Where did you meet this rather conceited and sometimes charming young man?"

"In Northumberland."

"*Northumberland!* I see—or rather, I do not see. Is your home in Northumberland?"

"Yes, my lord."

"Do not tell me that you have come all the way from Northumberland to Kensington and then from Kensington to here in pursuit of Mr. Drew? You did not walk *all* the way, I trust."

She blushed deeply. "I daresay it must look very— very peculiar to you, sir. But I am not exactly in pursuit of him—at least, not in the way you must think—"

"You mean that you are not in love with him."

"No. Indeed, no!"

"There is no need to be so vehement, Miss Spencer. I can see very well that you are not the type of young woman to run after any young man, however handsome, for such a reason." He looked down at his hand, with its fine and well-manicured fingers. "I wonder, then, what motive is powerful enough to bring you so many miles? If it is not love, it must be revenge."

"Not really, my lord. I hope I am not a vengeful person—though I believe Mr. Drew may have deceived me unpardonably. It is very hard to explain without telling you the whole story."

"Then I suggest that you do," he said quietly. "You may count on my discretion absolutely. And if Mr. Drew has wronged you, I can assure you that you have come to the very person to see that the wrong is redressed."

Again Katherine hesitated, and again, for the same reasons as before, she finally decided to speak.

"It may bore you, my lord."

"On the contrary," he said with a small smile. "I think I shall be most interested."

She took a deep breath. "My father, Sir Roland Spencer, died some years ago, and the baronetcy and our family home in Northumberland went to my elder brother, Harry." She paused. "Unfortunately, Harry did not care as much as he should for Kielder—"

"What did you say the name of your home is?"

"Kielder, sir. Kielder Castle. It is very old and has been in our family for nearly five hundred years. It is not quite as it once was, in the old days, but it is still a very fine place."

"I can see that you, at any rate, do not share your brother's indifference to your ancestral home. Pray continue."

"Harry became very bored with life there. It *is* very quiet, you see. There is no Society or entertainment—only the Spencer Arms, and even that is three miles away. *I* do not mind at all myself, but I can understand how Harry found it so hard to be content. He loved company, you see, and—"

"There is no need to excuse your brother. I follow perfectly."

"A year ago Harry came to London. It was what he had always wanted. He lived very recklessly, I am afraid, and spent nearly all his inheritance; the remainder he gambled away, I believe."

"Sir Harry Spencer," the earl mused. "I may have come across him at one or other of the clubs, I fancy. A large-built, dark-haired young man of about two and twenty, with a somewhat loud voice and an even louder laugh?"

"It sounds like Harry," she admitted. "Or like he was. He was killed taking part in a race from London to Brighton. His curricle overturned on a bend."

"I am distressed to hear that. Please accept my condolences."

"Thank you." Katherine looked down at her glass. "Mr. Drew also took part in that race. In fact, he won."

"Really? In what time?"

"Four hours, forty minutes, I think he said," she answered, rather puzzled at the earl's interest.

"What delayed him, I wonder."

She looked at him in surprise. "Surely that is fast?"

He waved his hand gently. "It is of no importance, Miss Spencer. Please go on."

"Well, on the night before he died, my brother had been gambling at a club—White's, I believe it was called—in company with Mr. Drew. He lost very heavily, and having no money he then wrote vowels."

"A common enough practice."

She swallowed. "There was some kind of argument, it seems. Someone provoked Harry—implied he would not be able to meet his debts. He became very angry and, I think, had been drinking too much, so he did not know what he was doing."

"What did he do, Miss Spencer?"

"He staked Kielder . . . and lost. To Mr. Drew."

There was silence for a moment. The earl's face was expressionless, and Katherine could not tell if he was shocked or surprised or simply unconcerned. And indeed, she thought, why should he care? Kielder is nothing to him.

"What happened then?" the earl enquired.

"Mr. Drew came north to claim Kielder. I knew nothing of what Harry had done until then. I thought my young brother William now owned the castle."

"The new baronet?" His eyes softened in sympathy. "That must have been calamitous news for you."

"It was," she said simply. "But there was nothing to be done. I saw the voucher and there was no doubt that it was in my brother's writing. Harry even instructed his London lawyers to deliver the deeds of Kielder to Mr. Drew before he took part in the race."

"You say there was nothing to be done, but you seem to me to be a young woman of some resource and courage. I find it difficult to believe that you gave in meekly."

"Well, I did ask Mr. Drew if he would sell Kielder back to us."

"Forgive my impertinence, Miss Spencer, but had you the money to buy it?"

"If he had asked a low price, we might have managed. Both Will and I have legacies from our father."

"In short, you hoped to appeal to his conscience?"

"He has none, I am convinced of it. Or he would have torn up Harry's voucher in the first place. He had no *need* of Kielder. He has—or he *said* he had—two homes already."

"The one supposedly in South Audley Street and—ah—Cheynings? I take it that Mr. Drew refused to sell."

"Not precisely. He said he would consider the possibility and make up his mind by the end of this month."

"I see." The earl stroked his cheek gently. "And what was your response to this?"

"I decided to make life at Kielder as uncomfortable for him as possible—in the hope, of course, that he would decide he did not want it after all."

The earl gave a wintry smile. "And how did you achieve this?"

Miss Spencer, in some confusion, told him about the blocked chimney, the broken windows, and the hole in the roof.

"I was right," the earl observed when she had finished. "You *are* a young woman of resource and courage. And what was the effect of these desperate measures?"

"Nothing. Nothing at all. That was the strangest thing. He did not seem to *mind* the discomfort. Are you familiar with the North, sir?"

"A little."

"Then you will know that it is very different from the

South. It is beautiful and wild and—and *natural*. People from London generally consider it to be uncivilised, I believe, though I do not agree at all. There is quite as much which is uncivilised in London, so far as I can see. But there is no denying that Kielder *is* not at all comfortable, even at the best of times." She looked around her at the elegant saloon. "It is not at all like this. In fact, it could not be more dissimilar. I cannot understand how a gentleman from London like Mr. Drew could have found it at all to his taste."

"Has it occurred to you, Miss Spencer, that he might have found the circumstances, at least, highly entertaining? That he was diverted by your brave efforts to dislodge him? And, perhaps, that you yourself intrigued him? If he is as handsome as you say then he would not be accustomed to such spirited—opposition, shall we say—from women."

"I believe they usually fall at his feet, which must be very bad for him. I'm sure he was spoiled as a child."

"An interesting conjecture."

"His behaviour in London is said to be very wild; his father despairs of him."

"Really? Did he tell you that?"

"Oh, no. Mr. Lovell told me. I daresay you will have heard of *him*. His father is Sir John Lovell, from Hertfordshire—"

The earl raised his hand. "Do enlighten me, Miss Spencer, I beg you. I find myself bewildered. How and when does Mr. Lovell from Hertfordshire come into the story?"

"He came to Kielder with a party of Mr. Drew's London acquaintances."

"I see. The expression on your face tells me that you did not greatly care for these London acquaintances."

"No, I did not. Except for Mr. Lovell," she said frankly. "*He* was very pleasant, but the rest were arrogant and ill-mannered, in my opinion. They had too high an opinion of themselves, though I daresay they were important in London and very grand. Nothing pleased them at Kielder, of course."

"I rather doubted it would."

"The gentlemen were better behaved than the ladies. Lady Beverly was quite odious . . . Are you acquainted with her, my lord? If so, I am sorry to speak ill of her."

"There is no need to be. Who else was present?"

"A Mr. and Mrs. de Vere."

"Ah! And how did you contrive to support these ill-mannered and arrogant acquaintances of Mr. Drew?"

"As well as I could, sir. I hope I was tolerably well behaved towards them, although at times they were most provoking. Especially Lady Beverly." Miss Spencer bit her lower lip. "I suppose I should not have dressed up as Lady Harriet."

"Again, I find myself confused. *Who* is Lady Harriet? Was she also one of the party?"

Katherine explained and was obliged to relate, some-what reluctantly, the affair of the ghost. The earl, listening, helped himself again to snuff, and once more the manner of his doing so seemed oddly familiar. When she had finished the tale he smiled, and for the first time the smile reached his eyes.

"I imagine that cured Lady Beverly of some of her arrogance."

She smiled too. "Yes, it did. She was rather quiet for a long time after it."

"And Mr. Drew never gave your secret away?"

"Never."

"That, at least, must have recommended him to you."

She shook her head. "I do not know what to say about it, my lord. He was full of strange contradictions. I could not discover what kind of a person he really was. He seems the complete dandy, and yet he hunts and shoots as well as any countryman I know. And he is very well read, which is even more surprising. He spent a great deal of time in the library at Kielder, where there is a very fine collection of books, and yet to see him you would not think him ever to have opened a single one!"

"You interest me more and more, Miss Spencer. And what happened after Lady Harriet frightened Lady Beverly out of her wits?"

"The snow melted, and soon after they all returned to London. Mr. Drew went with them but said he would return to Kielder before the end of the month."

"But you followed him to London. Why?"

"I had come to suspect that there was something mysterious about him. Lady Beverly and the others acted very oddly, you see, sir, as though there was some secret between them about him. And I overheard Lord Beverly call him Melvin once—which seemed peculiar, to say the least, as his name is Richard."

"And so you travelled all the way from Northumberland to discover the truth about Mr. Drew? Your persistence and courage is greatly to be admired, Miss Spencer. I felicitate you."

"You see, my lord, if he is not who he pretended to be, then he may have no right to Kielder after all."

"And Kielder means a great deal to you, does it not?"

"Everything."

He rose from his chair and went to the bellpull. Then he looked down at her for a moment before he said slowly, "Kielder will be restored to you, Miss Spencer. You may set your mind at rest. There is no need for you to trouble yourself further."

She stared up at him. "But how—how can you help? How can you know, my lord?"

"You will see in a moment, my dear."

The butler answered his master's summons, and the earl spoke to him in a brief aside. Miss Spencer waited nervously. She wished very much now that she had kept silent. It had been a mistake to pour out her troubles to a stranger. What stupidity! What foolishness! How could she have been so indiscreet! How could she have been so—

The door opened again and Mr. Drew walked into the room.

In the silence that followed, the earl said smoothly, "Allow me to present my son and, unfortunately, my heir, Lord Melvin—though I doubt if it will afford you any great pleasure." He took Katherine's hand in his and bowed over it gracefully. "It has been an honour to meet you, Miss Spencer. It is not every day that I encounter a woman who is the match of my son. I shall leave you to deal with him as he deserves. Punish him as you think fit for the absurd charade he has played on you, and be assured that you have no further cause for alarm."

He left the room with the coldest of nods towards his heir. Miss Spencer had risen to her feet and stood beside the settee in agitation. The shock of seeing Mr. Drew so unexpectedly, followed by the revelation of his real identity, had left her speechless. An earl's son . . . good heavens, that must mean he was a viscount! She saw now the resemblance he bore to his father and wondered how she could have been so blind. And she saw, too, that although she herself was in a fluster, *he* appeared quite undisturbed by the situation and was even daring to smile at her!

"I am very flattered, Miss Spencer, that you should have followed me all the way from Northumberland. How did you find me?"

Miss Spencer found her voice then. "I do not see how that is of any consequence, Mr. Drew—I mean, my lord. But if you must know, Mr. Lovell told me once that you lived in South Audley Street. And I followed you only to find out the truth."

He took a pinch of snuff, handling it exactly as his father had done. "Did David give me away? He has too honest a nature to deceive anyone for long."

"Why did you do it?" she asked. "Why pretend to have won Kielder from my brother? It was monstrous!"

"I did not pretend, Miss Spencer," he replied. "It *was* the truth. The night before your brother died the events were exactly as I described to you. Harry was at White's with me, and he staked Kielder and lost to me. However, I drank rather more than was good for me afterwards, and forgot everything about it until a week or so later, when your brother's lawyer delivered the deeds of Kielder to me. I might have torn up the voucher and returned the deeds, but that evening I was at a card party at the Beverlys and talked about it to David Lovell." He leaned his arm along the ledge of the chimneypiece and looked down into the fire for a moment. "Gambling is a fever, Miss Spencer. It takes all kinds of forms. People bet on flies crawling up a wall and on raindrops running down a window . . . all manner of nonsense. It is a compulsive vice without sense or reason. David bet fifty guineas that I would not go directly to Kielder, claim the castle under an assumed name, and keep up the pretence for one month. Harry had portrayed you as a most fearsome prospect, you remember, which added—er, zest, you might say, to the wager."

"So you accepted," she said witheringly.

"I seldom refuse a wager; it is a matter of honour."

"Of honour! How can you speak of *honour*!"

"It may not be honour as you understand it, Miss Spencer, but it is a kind of honour, nonetheless. Yes, I accepted the wager and assumed the name of my father's butler, which was the first I could think of. I hired a coach and drove north directly. The rest you already know."

"Too well!"

"And you are forgetting one thing," he went on, soft-voiced. "I won Kielder and I still own it. That is the truth."

He took the piece of paper he had shown her at Kielder from his pocket and held it, dangling lightly, between his fingers.

"Harry was drunk," she said despairingly. "He did not know what he was doing."

"You delude yourself. Harry knew perfectly well what he was doing. And Harry didn't give a damn!"

Miss Spencer was silent for a moment. Detestable man! He had spoken the truth, but it was no more welcome to her than if it had been more lies.

"Very well. You still own Kielder. Perhaps you will tell me now if you are prepared to sell it back to us?"

"Yes," he said. "For a price."

"What price? I have not a great deal of money—"

"I am prepared to be generous. More than generous." He looked at the piece of paper consideringly. "Well now, let me see . . . what shall I ask? I know. One kiss from you, Miss Spencer, and Kielder is yours again."

"One—one *what*?"

"Is the price too high for you? One, not a dozen, I said."

"This is absurd. There is no need to make a joke of it."

"I am perfectly serious," he told her. "One kiss from you is my price for Kielder. It seems very reasonable to me. Are you prepared to pay it or not?"

She glared at him. "This is your idea of amusement. I find it despicable! No wonder your father despairs of you! I am very sorry for him, having such a son. Very sorry indeed."

"I cannot see why you are so upset. It's not the first time, after all. In fact, it will be the third, to be precise. The only difference is that it will be the first time *you* have kissed me, instead of the other way round."

"Oh! You are intolerable! If I were a man—"

"Now it is you who are being absurd." He caught hold

143

of her wrist. "Come, you may as well pay and be done with it."

His grip was so strong that there seemed little chance of freeing herself. Katherine considered calling for help, and then her eyes fell again on the piece of paper in his other hand and on Harry's drunken scrawl.

"Your word that you will destroy the voucher?"

"My word on it." He smiled down at her. "Think of Will and Kielder."

She did so resolutely and kissed him shyly on the cheek.

"That's not what I meant," he said laughingly. "That wouldn't pay for the drawbridge."

He pulled her into his arms. The touch of his lips was light at first but as the kiss went on and on it became more and more demanding, until Katherine was lost to every thought—even that of Will and Kielder. Her bonnet slid back from her head and hung loose by its ribbons, and his fingers entwined themselves in her hair, holding her prisoner. When at last he let her go, she retrieved her bonnet and retied it with very unsteady fingers, whilst without a word he tore the voucher in half and tossed the pieces into the fire, where they flared brightly before burning to nothing. Miss Spencer began to draw on her gloves hurriedly and moved towards the door.

"Leaving so soon?" he enquired politely, as though nothing had happened. "Where are you putting up in London?"

With her back to him, she replied coldly, "With Miss Lorrimer's aunt, Mrs. Jennings, in Kensington."

"Don't tell me that Miss Lorrimer is also come down from Northumberland?"

"She is."

"Then David will be overjoyed to hear it! He has been mooning about like a lovesick calf ever since we returned to London."

Katherine, hearing this, turned round. "Is that really true?"

"Certainly. Why should you doubt it?"

She hesitated, then said, "Because poor Letty is quite convinced that he has been discouraged by her Connexion with Trade."

"Then she is sadly mistaken in him. It is *he* who feels himself unworthy of *her*, and is afraid of being thought a fortune hunter."

"Oh dear! What a misunderstanding! And I am convinced they are so suited."

"I agree. We could play cupid, if you wish. I shall undertake to bring David to call on Mrs. Jennings in Kensington. And we could each tell them what the other is really thinking."

For Letty's sake, Katherine could only agree—although it would mean seeing the viscount again, and just at that moment she felt it to be the last thing on earth she wanted. Despite her protests, he insisted on sending for the carriage to take her back to Kensington, and she journeyed there in the utmost style and comfort. Her thoughts, however, were in disorder, and anything but comfortable. She no longer seemed to be able to think straight about things, and from time to time she touched her lips with her fingers. There was one fact, at least, that she could seize upon joyfully and thankfully— Kielder belonged to Will now. The voucher was burned to ashes. The castle had been restored to the Spencers again. She had a vague suspicion, though, that somehow the price she had paid for this might prove higher than she had imagined.

9

MRS. JENNINGS AND Letty were returning from their shopping expedition at the same time as the carriage bearing Miss Spencer drew up at the door, and their mouths opened in astonishment. It was ill luck for Katherine, who was then obliged to recount her own outing, and although she did so as briefly as possible she could not conceal the importance of the carriage. Mrs. Jennings's sharp eyes had instantly spotted the crest painted on the door, and any reservations she might have had about her guest sallying forth alone and unchaperoned in London were quickly dispelled, and even the day's purchases forgotton in her eagerness to discover the owner of such magnificence. When she learned who it was her mouth opened even wider.

"The Earl of Ingram, my dear! Good gracious! Upon my soul, I can scarcely credit it! He must be one of the richest men in England, and the family goes back to the Norman Conquest, if not further. Their town house is near the park, is it not? Yes, I thought so. And then, of course, there is Cheynings. Now *that* is one of the finest houses in the country. Lady Mablethorpe has stayed there once herself, and says it is the most beautiful place she has ever set eyes on. The gardens are perfection!"

"Cheynings?" said Letty, looking at Katherine. "Did you say *Cheynings*?"

"Indeed I did, my love. The country seat of the earls of Ingram," Mrs. Jennings replied with satisfaction.

"Surely you must have heard of it: it is quite famous, you know. What good fortune that Miss Spencer should be acquainted with such distinguished company! And the heir, Viscount Melvin, is one of the most eligible bachelors in London. *Everyone* has been trying to ensnare him, but he is a trifle wild and will not be caught, not even by the greatest beauties. Arabella Chesney was quite *distraught* when he did not marry her after flirting with her for a whole Season! His exploits are common gossip." Mrs. Jennings lowered her voice to a loud whisper. "Why, only a few months ago, it was all round town that he had killed a man in a duel! And he is always to be found at the gaming clubs, and it is nothing for him to play for twenty-four hours at a sitting. He has been known to lose five hundred pounds an hour and then win it all back again the next night. I believe he is a very fine whip—one of the best there is—and, of course, he has ridden at Newmarket himself. . . ."

She rambled on happily in this way for some while, and when she had finished there was little that they did not know about the Ingram family or the indiscretions of its heir. A French actress, the wife of a duke, the Spanish ambassador's daughter had all, it seemed, been his *chères amies* at one time or another, and it was rumoured, though it was probably a libellous falsehood, that the youngest Mountjoy looked remarkably like him . . .

Letty's eyes grew rounder and rounder as she listened, and she kept darting enquiring glances at Katherine, who was very busy looking out of the window. Later, when they were alone and safely out of Mrs. Jennings's earshot, she demanded to know everything.

"Good God! Do you mean to say that Mr. Drew and Lord Melvin are the same person," she said in amazement. "How extraordinary! But then I always told you, Kate, did I not, that he was of the very first style and consequence? You must admit it! And you say it was all for a wager? And he has torn up and burned the voucher? Why are you blushing, Kate?"

"I am not."

"Yes, you are, but never mind. I own I cannot approve of what he did, nor of Mr. Lovell's part in it—though I am sure *he* did not mean any harm—but a viscount, Kate! I wish I had known, for I have never met one before!"

"Then you will meet one again, Letty, for Lord Melvin has promised to bring Mr. Lovell to call here."

"Oh!"

"He says you are quite wrong to doubt him; he has been lovesick for you ever since they left Kielder, and it is *not* your Connexion that has discouraged him at all, but that he is only a younger son with little to his name, whilst you are an heiress. He is very much afraid of being thought a fortune hunter."

"Oh, how foolish of him! And how noble! As if I should ever think that."

"Then you will have to convince him of it. It does not matter, of course, what anyone else may think."

"Except Papa," said Letty, momentarily dampened. "You know how he can be. No one is good enough for me. He is always very rude about poor Vernon."

"Vernon and Mr. Lovell are not at all the same thing."

"No, that is very true. But still . . ." Letty brightened suddenly. "*You* must speak to Papa for us, Kate. He will listen to you. He always does. *You* could persuade him that Mr. Lovell is the kindest, most noble creature alive, who will make me the best husband in the world!"

Katherine laughed. "You had better wait until he offers for you."

"Do not worry," said Letty. "I shall *make* him!"

The following day Lord Melvin and Mr. Lovell called at the Kensington house. Mrs. Jennings, perceiving the carriage from the front window and watching the two gentlemen descend, was in transports of delight.

"So handsome! So elegant! Such style and such an air!"

It was not clear precisely which gentleman she was referring to, or whether it was to both, but when they entered the room it was apparent that, although Mr. Lovell received a most courteous welcome, it was Lord Melvin who commanded the greater share of her admiration and attention. He did, indeed, present a very handsome and striking figure in a blue coat, buff-coloured waistcoat, deep stiff white cravat, and buckskin breeches worn with shining hessians. Mrs. Jennings, enjoying herself immensely, engaged him at once in a spirited exchange of gossip and news. To have one of the leaders of Society, however wild, under her roof was an opportunity not to be missed on any account, and since his lordship was kind enough to indulge her thirst for titbits, the widow made full use of the occasion. It was true that since the Season had not yet begun there was a paucity of events, but nevertheless she had heard some intriguing *on dits* lately that required verification.

"Do tell me," she whispered behind her hand to him, "is it true that Lady Longman has run off with her footman? I hear they have fled to France, and Lord Longman is threatening to shoot himself if she does not return."

"The first part is certainly true," he replied. "As to the second, it is the footman his lordship is threatening to shoot, and he is already consoling himself with the Countess of Weston."

Mrs. Jennings was enchanted. She bent a little closer. "And what of Lord Worsham? They do say he is already tiring of his wife, although they have only been married six months, and that Mrs. Ramsay is frequently to be seen on his arm of late. . . ."

She continued in this vein for some time, whilst Letty

and Mr. Lovell, happily reunited, conversed together on the settee. Miss Lorrimer looked charming in a new gown of palest blue, and her hair had grown enough to curl prettily about her face. It was no wonder that Mr. Lovell looked bewitched. Katherine, left in limbo, sat alone, not liking to listen or to join in either conversation. She took up some embroidery to occupy herself, and looked up once to encounter the viscount's eyes fixed upon her. This so forcibly reminded her of their last meeting that thereafter she kept her own eyes down upon her work. At length, Mrs. Jennings became gradually aware that his lordship's attention was wandering, and in which direction, and generously sacrificed several more topics that she had in mind for discussion. She rose to her feet and called upon Miss Spencer to take her place whilst she oversaw the arrangements for some refreshments, since the servants could not be trusted.

"You have not yet told me how you like London," he said pleasantly as she sat down beside him. "What is your impression of the city?"

"I have seen too little of it," she replied, plying her needle. "I cannot make any proper judgement. The poverty is quite shocking, and there is much that is very ugly, but there is also a great deal that is very beautiful."

"There is indeed, and I should be honoured if you would allow me to show it to you. London is the most fascinating city in the world."

"That is kind of you, my lord, but I shall be returning to Kielder shortly."

"Then you should not leave without seeing as much as possible, or you will carry away as false an impression of the South as Lady Beverly did of the North."

"Is her ladyship in town at present?"

"Fortunately, no. Beverly has removed her to their country home—much against her will. The de Veres have gone to keep her company, lest she die of boredom. So you are quite safe from them."

"But you have not gone to the country, Lord Melvin. Is that because you, too, are likely to die of boredom?"

"Not at all. As you know, I can amuse myself in the country quite as well as in town, but family affairs keep me in town for the next day or two. In other circumstances, of course, I should have been returning to Kielder almost immediately." He smiled as she coloured. "One day, I shall hope to show you Cheynings, Miss Spencer. It is as beautiful as your home, but in a very different way: it is mellow where Kielder is rugged and ordered where Kielder is wild. I think you would like it, although it lacks the drama of your castle—and there are no dungeons."

"I'm sure it is lovely," she said, pinker still.

"Meanwhile," he continued, "I shall have to content myself with showing you something of London. I shall make an excellent guide, I promise you. I shall call for you tomorrow morning at eleven and we shall make a grand tour."

"I do hope you will not be so foolish as to agree, Miss Spencer," Mr. Lovell called to her across the room. "Richard drives like the very devil. Beware of him!"

"Take no notice," the viscount replied. "He is piqued because he can never beat me. He has no eye for horseflesh and the worst hands imaginable. You will be quite safe with me."

Mr. Lovell laughed. "Don't believe him, I beg you, Miss Spencer."

"David, if you do not stop trying to put Miss Spencer off, I shall be obliged to call you out," his lordship replied good-humouredly. "It is all settled, in any case. I am calling for her tomorrow morning."

Refreshments were brought in at that moment and Katherine had no further opportunity to argue. Lord Melvin was soon reclaimed by Mrs. Jennings and remained in conversation with her for the rest of the visit; she almost suspected him of deliberately denying her the chance of refusal. She could not understand why he should wish to drive her out and wondered if it were part of some prearranged plan in order that Mr. Lovell might be alone with Letty; certainly, there had been some private meaning behind the look she had seen exchanged between the two men. Well, if that was the reason, then she could not refuse anything which might procure Letty's happiness. And besides, she told herself rationally, she really *would* like to see something of London before she returned north. The chance to do so might never come her way again, and if it had to be in the company of Mr. Drew—she still could not bring herself to *think* of him as Lord Melvin—then she must just make the best of it.

The viscount arrived the next morning promptly at eleven o'clock, and Miss Spencer presented herself dociley enough. It was a fine and sunny day, despite the season, and the curricle-and-four that awaited her outside with a liveried groom was the raciest-looking, most dashing vehicle she had ever seen. Remembering Mr. Lovell's warning, she eyed it with some trepidation, but there was no going back. His lordship had taken her arm firmly and handed her up into the carriage. He tucked a rug about her knees, and Katherine, who was quite unused to such attentions, felt a little gratified at being thus pampered. He climbed up beside her, the groom released the wheelers and scrambled up behind them, and they moved off. As they bowled along the street at a brisk but controlled pace, she could not help being aware of the distinction of driving out in such style, nor could she fail to notice how superbly Lord Melvin handled the chestnuts. Once or twice she glanced at him as he sat with his hands lightly but surely on the reins; she decided that there must be at least a dozen capes to his grey driving coat and that his hat must be beaver. If he noticed her inspection, however, he gave no sign of it.

"It is very tedious of you to be quite so skilled at everything," she remarked after a while, when he had just negotiated with fine accuracy a narrow passageway between a dray and a coach. "Is there anything you *cannot* do, I wonder?"

He turned briefly to her with a smile. "A great deal, I assure you. For instance, I cannot make you like me."

"Does that matter?"

"I am not accustomed to failure, where women are concerned."

"Then it is very good for you. But with an earldom and a fortune to come, I doubt it will occur many times in your life."

"Would you prefer that I was still plain Mr. Drew?" he asked, his attention on guiding the chestnuts past a cartload of hay.

"It makes no difference to me," she answered.

He smiled again, but this time to himself. "I rather thought not."

He drove her down Birdcage Walk and past the Queen's House. Katherine was disappointed by the ordinariness of the red brick and stone building with its semicircular sweep of iron rails in the front. It looked shabby and dull and scarcely a fit place for a royal residence. The poor, mad King she knew to be at Windsor, where, as Mrs. Jennings had told them—and on the best authority—he wandered about in a violet dressing gown with the Star of the Order of the Garter pinned to his chest, a blind old man with a long white beard.

They bowled down the Mall in St. James's Park and passed by the palace of Carlton House, hidden behind its screen of pillars. He reined in the horses so that she might catch more than a glimpse of the fine building with its great portico of six columns, surmounted by a frieze and adorned by the arms of the Prince Regent.

"Whatever else he may be, nobody can deny that Prinny is a man of style. The interior is magnificent." Katherine considered the home of the heir to the throne. "Is he not also said to be very extravagant, very fat, and very wicked?"

"He is also very charming and has excellent taste."

"Does that excuse his faults?" she asked, smiling.

"No, but it makes them easier to forgive."

They drove on to Westminster Abbey, and here they alighted, leaving the groom to walk the horses whilst they went inside. Katherine was instantly beguiled. Within these ancient walls, she thought as she looked about her, fascinated, all the kings and queens of England since William the Conqueror have been crowned, and many of them are buried here too. Their bones still lie here, ghosts of England's history. Henry the Seventh, the first Tudor, lies here with his Yorkist queen, and Elizabeth herself is entombed in this place, not far from Mary Queen of Scots—the two queens meeting in death at last, as they had never done in life.

They looked at the shrine of Edward the Confessor. The tomb of the royal saint was encircled by other royal tombs—those of Henry II and the warlike Edward I, with his beloved Eleanor of Castile at his feet.

"And there lies the man who gave Kielder to your ancestors," her guide told her.

Katherine stared for a moment at the tomb of Edward III, the mighty and magnificent warrior king who had rewarded the loyalty of the Spencers in the far distant north of his kingdom so long ago. . . .

She was shown the tombs of Richard II and of Henry V, the victor of Agincourt, and the Coronation Chair on which all these monarchs had been crowned.

Later, they went out into the old gardens of the abbey.

"This was once a Benedictine monastery," he said. "It began as a few monks living in a group of mud huts round a small stone chapel on a marshy island, and grew into a great monastery, endowed by Edward the Confessor and ruled over by powerful abbots."

As they walked, she listened to her guide with interest, and the irony of the fact that this was the same man who had talked with Mrs. Jennings of idle gossip with equal authority did not escape her. It was not hard to imagine the abbot's orchards, vineyards, and fishponds, which had once been close by—so strong was the sense of monastic shade and stillness.

They continued their tour, driving eastwards along the north bank of the river, and he pointed out Lambeth Palace and the towers and spires of Southwark on the far bank. Between lay the wide and muddy expanse of the Thames, swift-flowing, perilous, and timeless.

"See that boat in midstream," he said, indicating it with his whip. "That is the horse ferry. It is still used, despite the bridges. Do you know that when King James the Second quitted Whitehall he came here and crossed the river at this very spot, to where horses were waiting for him on the other side at Vauxhall, ready to take him to France. He went in a small boat with a single pair of oars and took with him the Great Seal of England, and as he crossed he threw it overboard into the water."

Katherine was horrified. "So it was lost forever?"

"Oh, no," he replied. "It was recovered later, quite by chance. It was caught up in the net of some poor fishermen, who delivered it into the hands of the Lords of the Council."

"I am vastly relieved to hear it," she said, looking back over her shoulder.

They continued along Millbank, round the bend in the river, and so on up Ludgate Hill to St. Paul's. The cathedral rose before them at the top of the hill, its great dome shining brightly in the sun and presenting a complete contrast to the ancient abbey. It was light, spacious, and elegant. They climbed up high to the Whispering Gallery.

"How does it work?" she asked, curious.

"Stay there," he told her. "I shall whisper something to you from the other side, and my voice will travel round to you so that you will be able to hear every word I say."

She waited, and when he had reached the far side of the gallery, he stopped and looked across at her.

> *"Such wilt thou be to me, who must*
> *Like the other foot, obliquely run;*
> *Thy firmness makes my circle just,*
> *And makes me end where I begun."*

He had whispered very low, but she could hear what he said as plainly as if he stood next to her; she blushed and was glad he was not so near. When he returned to her side, she asked him who had written the verse.

"John Donne. He was Dean of St. Paul's two hundred years ago." He smiled. "So it seemed fitting."

After they had left the cathedral they drove through some of the narrow streets and hilly lanes of old London: Cornhill, Gracechurch Street, Eastcheap, Mincing Lane, Fenchurch Street—where he showed her the Elephant Tavern which had been spared in the Great Fire, although everything else about it had been destroyed—and thence to Pudding Lane, where the fire had begun, and to the monument on Fish Street Hill which commemorated the terrible event.

The Tower of London was all that she had always imagined it to be: gloomy, sinister, grim. Even the sunshine could not dispel the aura of menace and tragedy that hung about its moated walls. Katherine thought with a shiver of the poor wretches who had been incarcerated there without justice or hope before their execution on the block—Lady Jane Grey, Anne Boleyn,

Catherine Howard, Thomas Seymour, Thomas More . . . Their misery still seemed to hang upon the air. The collection of wild beasts did nothing to lift her spirits, since she found no pleasure in seeing animals kept captive, and she was glad when they left the Tower and drove westwards, via Charing Cross. Her guide swung the curricle down King Street, where he pointed out the entrance to Almack's, the exclusive temple, as she learned, of the *beau monde*, the gates of which were guarded by lady patronesses whose smiles or frowns consigned aspirants to happiness or despair, as the case might be.

He turned down St. James's Street and stopped outside an impressive building fronted by tall columns rising from the first floor to the roof, and with a flight of steps leading up to the main door. In the centre, a large bow window overlooked the street, and Katherine could see a number of very elegantly attired dandies lounging therein.

"White's," the viscount told her. "The club where your brother was so imprudent."

She looked up at the place where Harry had gambled away Kielder, and thought sadly of him. It was easy to see why he had frequented it so much. The gentlemen in the window looking down at them were just such as he would have wished to associate with. Several more had now joined the group: one of them raised his hand in greeting while another pressed forward to see better.

"Do they always stare out of the window like that?"

"They are wondering who you are."

"Oh!"

"Take no notice of them," he reassured her, and to her relief he allowed the restless chestnuts to move on.

"Have you heard of Beau Brummel?" he asked as they drove round Berkeley Square.

"The Prince Regent's great friend? Yes, indeed. Letty has told me many times how he is the leader of all fashion, and how a single word from him may decide the fate of anyone wishing to be launched into Society. I feel sure he must be a very opinionated sort of person and quite as bad as your patronesses."

"There you are wrong. He is quite the contrary. It is the opinion of others that has awarded him such arbitrary powers. He himself is modest and good-natured. I have never seen him in ill humour, and he is the most agreeable and amusing conversationalist. You would like him."

"You must be well acquainted with him to know so much about him."

"I am indeed acquainted with him. That is Lady Jersey's house, by the way—number thirty-eight. She is one of the patronesses of Almack's. There is a story told of Beau Brummell that he was walking through this square at five o'clock one summer's morning, lamenting his ill fortune at cards, when he saw something glittering on the pavement. He stooped down and picked up a crooked sixpence, thinking it must be a harbinger of good luck. He took it home, drilled a hole through it, and fastened it to his watch chain."

"And did it bring him good luck?"

"For more than two years after, he was a constant winner at play and on the turf, to the sum of nearly thirty thousand pounds!"

"Then it did bring him good fortune! No doubt he needed it, though. To be a leader of fashion must call for well-lined pockets."

"It does," he said drily. "Beau's boots are polished with champagne!"

"What a dreadful waste!" she exclaimed, not sure whether to believe him. "Where are we going now?"

"Hyde Park. The place where the fashionables ride and drive and walk—at certain well-prescribed times of the day, of course—to see and be seen by the rest of their kind."

They entered by the gate at the Corner and went down the Drive. As he had forewarned, the park was full of persons of rank and fashion, all observing each other, and the viscount's curricle-and-four, Katherine noted, received a good deal more than its fair share of attention. Scarcely a carriage or a rider or a walker passed by without a salutation of some kind, accompanied by a penetrating look at herself.

"You seem to know a great many people in London," she said, after they had encountered a stylish young gentleman, on an equally stylish grey horse, who had somehow contrived to execute an elegant bow to Katherine from his saddle.

"I do," he replied briefly.

She turned her head to see that the young gentleman was still staring after them.

"Your friend is still watching you. How ill-mannered of him!"

"It is you that he is watching, not me. He is curious— like the gentlemen at White's—to know who you are."

"Whatever for?"

"There is nothing more enjoyable to them than gossip," he said. "They love to speculate on this or that. If I am seen driving through the park with an unknown lady at my side, they will not rest until they discover who she is. Depend upon it, they will contrive somehow to find you out, and within the next few days rumours of our imminent betrothal will be circulating London."

"But that is ridiculous!"

"Isn't it?" he agreed, sending the chestnuts smoothly past a slow-moving *vis-à-vis* carriage containing two elderly dowagers who raised their eyeglasses in unison to stare as hard as the rest. "But you need not let it worry you. I shall deny it emphatically!"

"Thank you."

"Not at all."

"It must be very annoying to be married off to every female you drive out with," she said, after a moment or two.

"Sometimes it is," he replied. "But not always." He turned his head towards her, and there was a look in his eyes that made the riposte she had been going to give die on her lips. She was silent, until the sight of a bright pink shell-shaped carriage approaching made her gasp with amazement.

"Whatever is that?"

"That," he said, "is Romeo Coates."

Miss Spencer stared in disbelief at the oncoming cockleshell drawn by two white horses. The harness and every available part of the extraordinary vehicle was emblazoned with the device of golden cockerels crowing. To her amusement, the equipage was escorted by several small and ragged boys, who ran beside the wheels crying "Cock-a-doodle-do!" at the tops of their voices. The occupant of the carriage—a well-dressed, dusky gentleman wearing a great quantity of fur—took no account of these appendages but smiled and bowed from left to right as he proceeded on his way.

"He is called Romeo," Lord Melvin explained, "because he played that part for one night only at the theatre in the Haymarket. Everyone went to see him."

"He scarcely looks the part!"

The viscount smiled. "He turned tragedy into comedy, though not intentionally. I was there myself. He is of West Indian extraction and exceedingly wealthy—but no actor, as you can imagine. He wore a cloak of blue silk, profusely spangled, red pantaloons, and a wig of the style of Charles the Second—all capped by an opera hat! He brought the whole house down with laughter before he even opened his mouth. And, to make matters worse, or still better, his nether garments were far too tight, and the seams split! I have never seen *Romeo and Juliet* better received by an audience! His absurd rendering of the balcony scene had the gallery and pit convulsed and the piece ended in uproar! Your tour of London would not have been complete without witnessing the spectacle of Romeo Coates on his daily drive through the park!"

Katherine laughed aloud at this tale and looked back to watch the ridiculous sight for a while.

He halted a little further on and proposed that they should walk across to the Serpentine River. Although they were in London, they might have been in deep country, so pastoral was the scene of cows and deer grazing beneath the trees. They strolled along beside the water's edge, but after a moment or two Miss Spencer wrinkled her nose and grimaced.

"It is perhaps better admired from a distance," he said drily. "It is artificial. Several ponds and pools were turned into this river, which is not a river and which, despite its name is almost straight. Unfortunately, the result has been fifty acres of stagnant water, fed by sewers—pleasant to the eye but offensive to the nose!"

He led her to a path a little away from the bank, and paused, leaning on an ancient oak.

"Last winter the Serpentine froze over," he told her, "and there was a fair held here on the ice. It is a very popular place for skating. I once drove a coach-and-four across from one side to the other for a wager." He looked at her quizzically. "I told you that some people will take wagers on almost anything."

"No wonder your father despairs of you!"

"I remind him too well of his own misspent youth, that is why. He was greatly taken by you, Miss Spencer. I think he sees in you the possibility of my salvation."

"Oh, dear. He will be disappointed, then."

"My mother and sister would love you, too. You will meet them when you come to visit Cheynings."

"Unfortunately, I shall not have that pleasure, sir. I shall be returning to Kielder very soon."

"But not yet," he said with a smile. "I shall not let you go yet."

To change the subject, she pointed to where several coaches were driving in slow and stately fashion round and round a clump of trees, and asked him what they were doing. Some were driving round in one direction and others the opposite way, which produced a rather pretty, if odd, effect. After they had driven like that for some time they turned round and drove in the opposite direction.

"That is the Ring," he told her. "A fashionable meeting place still, although part of it was destroyed in making the Serpentine. It is also well known for the duels that have taken place there in the past."

She looked up at him. "It is said that you killed a man in a duel. Is that true?"

"Who told you that? Mrs. Jennings, I suppose. We fought with swords and I wounded him—that is all. The affair was concluded amicably."

"How barbarous! Could it not have been settled without fighting?"

He smiled. "No wonder my father approves of you!"

They walked back towards the carriage by a parallel path. A large puddle of water blocked the way ahead, and before she could protest he had lifted her and carried her across.

"Would you kindly put me down, sir!"

"In a moment," he said, striding on. "Do you object so much? It is not the first time I have carried you or held you in my arms, if you recall."

"*If* you please . . . !"

He set her down, laughing.

"Your boots are spoiled, my lord, which serves you right!"

"I do not care about my boots, Miss Spencer—as you should know by now."

He drove her back to Kensington, where the twitching

of the curtains at the front windows warned Katherine that Mrs. Jennings was watching eagerly. He handed her down from the carriage and kissed her hand.

"I shall see you at Lady Mablethorpe's tomorrow evening," he promised her.

There was no escaping the interrogation of Mrs. Jennings, who wished to know every detail of the tour. Letty was equally enthusiastic but less pressing, since she saw that Katherine was reluctant to speak much of it. Mr. Lovell had called again that morning, and her own happiness had made her anxious for her friend's: it was clear to her that poor Kate was in a state of confusion and uncertainty and wished only to be left alone. Letty was unable to prevent her aunt, however, from rhapsodising at length on the good looks and elegance of Lord Melvin, his probable income, his pedigree, the gardens at Cheynings, the mansion in South Audley Street, and the happy circumstance of his paying such very *marked* attention to Miss Spencer.

"Of course, my dear, it is well known that he is a most accomplished flirt, but I own there is something in his manner towards you which leads me to suspect—to hope—that he may have a serious *tendre* for you."

Katherine had grown quieter and quieter, and at this remark rose from her seat and begged to be excused, as she had a headache. In the silence of her bedchamber she sat for a long time, thinking. It required a very great deal of honest soul-searching before she could admit to herself that not only had she overcome her dislike of Lord Melvin, she had come to like him very much indeed. She could not give the precise moment when this bewildering change of heart and mind had taken place: it had come upon her by stealth somewhere between Westminster Abbey and the Tower . . . perhaps in the Whispering Gallery at St. Paul's. She remembered that when she had looked across at him there it had been as though she were suddenly seeing him for the first time, no longer as an enemy to be bested but—and she forced herself to be honest—as a lover. She had gone with him today on sufferance only and found, unexpectedly, that she had enjoyed his company. More than that, she had been wonderfully happy. He had shown another side to his character than the cynical nonchalance he habitually affected. In fact, he had been everything that was agreeable: amusing, knowledgeable, attentive, charming . . . oh yes, how he had been charming! She smiled to herself at this thought, and then her smile faded quickly. The truth was that she was in dreadful danger of falling in love with him. Unless she was very careful she would be no different from all the other females in London who swooned at his feet, and that was too awful to contemplate! Mrs. Jennings's hopeful speculations she dismissed as ridiculous. The only mystery was why, when he had the pick of London, he should choose to flirt with herself. So, what was to be done? She considered not going to Lady Mablethorpe's but decided this would be cowardly, and besides, what harm was there in seeing him once again before she left?

The small gathering promised by Mrs. Jennings proved a very much larger and grander affair than anticipated. Lady Mablethorpe's drawing rooms in Mount Street were already crowded when they arrived. At the sight of so many of the *haut ton* collected together, Letty clutched at Katherine's arm, her courage nearly deserting her in spite of her new gown of white tulle, cut fashionably short enough to allow her small feet to peep out from beneath the hem, while her feathered headdress effectively disguised her still *un*fashionably short hair. Katherine, without such props to sustain her morale, was not so much nervous as apprehensive. She scanned the company for Lord Melvin, but there was no sign of him, or of Mr. Lovell.

Mrs. Jennings, resplendent and animated in puce satin bedecked with many frills, presented her protégées to their hostess. Lady Mablethorpe welcomed them politely but without great enthusiasm, a rapid glance having established them as of no particular consequence. Letty was allowed to be decorative and naively charming, but Katherine was dismissed as of no interest at all.

As they moved on to mingle with the assembly, Mrs. Jennings was presently accosted—there being no other word to describe it—by a formidable-looking dowager in black satin and pearls. She ignored both Katherine and Letty and, on Mrs. Jennings begging leave to present them, raised her eyeglass and inspected them from top to toe with a thoroughness that was both rude and unnecessary.

"From *Northumberland*, did you say? Didn't know anyone lived there. Only barbarians!"

Fortunately, before Miss Spencer could think of a reply, the dowager's fickle attention was taken by another victim, and she abandoned them as quickly as she had come.

"*That*," said Mrs. Jennings with satisfaction, "is the Duchess of Crewe!"

"She may be a duchess," said Letty, *sotto voce*, "But she is altogether abominable!"

Miss Spencer was about to agree wholeheartedly when she heard her name spoken and turned to find the Earl of Ingram before her. The resemblance to his son was enough to make her start, but seeing that he was alone, she soon collected herself sufficiently to curtsey in answer to his bow. She presented him to Mrs. Jennings and Letty, and some pleasant conversation ensued, which delighted the widow, before he drew her aside.

"Have you forgiven my son for what he did, Miss Spencer?"

"Forgiven, if not forgotten, sir."

"He does not deserve such good fortune, of course. If he had less charm he would be less easily forgiven." She looked up at him curiously. Behind the earl's cold condemnation of his heir she thought she detected a touch of pride.

"Did *you* accept wagers once, my lord?"

He smiled slowly. "Of all kinds, I regret to say."

"Did you ever drive a coach-and-four across the Serpentine when it was frozen over, for example?"

He raised his thin eyebrows. "The *Serpentine?* My dear Miss Spencer! Why, I drove a coach-and-*six* across the *Thames!*"

She laughed, and he, looking down at her, seemed about to say something else of a more serious nature, when he was hailed by a loud-voiced gentleman who insistently demanded his presence elsewhere. He bowed to her, excusing himself for the moment.

Other company soon presented itself in the shape of a trio of young captains in Hussar uniform; fresh from the Peninsula, they were very dashing and eager. Katherine listened dutifully to a long and detailed account of some military skirmish, accompanied by illustrative gestures, and had reached the point where the enemy were put to flight in no uncertain terms, when she saw Lord Melvin enter at the far end of the room. Watching how Lady Mablethorpe hurried forward and how others pressed about him, she was reminded of Mr. Lovell's words at Kielder: *Everyone in London fawns over him.* The Hussar captain now only received half her attention as she witnessed the truth of these words. The viscount was the centre of attention and bore it all with his languid charm. A stout and determined mama pushed her shy and beautiful daughter before him, and the girl—little more than a child—stood with her eyes upon the floor, until a few and obviously well-chosen words from his lordship induced her to look up with blushing adoration. Miss

Spencer observed this somewhat cynically, and as she did so he looked across at her and smiled. Despite all her good resolutions her heart seemed to turn over.

Presently he made his way across to her, pausing here and there to exchange a few words. When finally he reached her side he extricated her adroitly and summarily from the Peninsular War.

"Is Nicholas boring you to death? He makes the mistake of imagining that everyone else is as fascinated as himself by every military campaign since the Battle of Hastings."

"Not at all," she rejoined. "Captain Montague has been most interesting."

"Liar!" he said. "I could see from across the room that you were dying of ennui."

"What makes you suppose that I should find your conversation any more interesting, sir?"

"Conceit," he replied. "And certainty. It could not be less interesting than a skirmish in the Peninsula." He smiled at her. "How do you like your first glimpse of Society?"

She looked about her and saw that people were staring at them—amongst them the gentleman who had ridden past them in Hyde Park.

"I am not sure that Society has very good manners," she said. "I was taught that it was impolite to stare."

"They still don't know who you are."

"I think they are wondering why you are addressing someone of such small consequence when they are all clamouring for your favours. The Duchess of Crewe, for instance, just to your right, can scarcely credit her eyes that you should be talking to me at all! She believes Northumberland to be inhabited only by barbarians."

"I suppose she has already found time to insult you. Shall we give her a set-down?"

He turned and bowed towards the dowager, who,

interpreting this as an invitation, bore down on them at once, full of effusive phrases.

"Dear Lord Melvin! Delightful to see you returned to town! London is not the same without you, not the same at all. All kinds of people find their way into company these days, from the strangest places! I was saying to my daughter Caroline only yesterday how much we missed you. She is bringing her eldest out this Season. You know, Joanna. Such a dear, sweet child!" The duchess tapped the viscount playfully with her black fan. "*And* a beauty! Wait till you clap eyes on her!" She levelled her glass at him. "How's your dear mother? You've been at Cheynings, I collect?"

"No, in Northumberland, ma'am."

"Northumberland!" Her grace cast a sharp glance over her shoulder at Miss Spencer, whom she had contrived to exclude from the conversation by the simple expedient of turning her back to her. "Surely not *Northumberland*! Were you *obliged* to go there? I cannot think one would ever go there from choice. A most uncivilised place, from all accounts. *You* must have found it so."

"Not at all," he said pleasantly. "I found it infinitely more civilised than London. In fact, I would recommend a long sojourn in Northumberland to anyone wishing to learn how to behave in civilised Society. You should try it, ma'am; it would benefit you enormously."

He bowed to her again and turned away to Katherine. The duchess glared through her glass, unable now to believe her ears as well as her eyes. Then, with an indignant heave of her massive pearl-laden bosom, she stalked away.

"Her grace is not at all pleased. You were not very polite."

"It was no more than she deserved. She is quite as rude to everyone she meets. Perhaps it may teach her a lesson, though I doubt it." He took her arm. "Let me find you somewhere to sit, and then I will fetch you a glass of wine."

He took her through the crowd, and their progress was attended by turning heads and whispered comments. He ignored them all and found her a chair in a small anteroom, leaving her there to fetch the wine. Katherine sat down, thankful to be away from the heat and the press. The only other occupants of the room were two ladies much too absorbed in their own conversation to pay her any regard. Seated together on a sofa, they were clearly busily engaged in demolishing the reputation of a third. The words *scandalous* and *disgraceful* reached her several times. She was engaged in examining a painting on the wall behind her of a tall ship wallowing in an exceedingly rough, green sea, when Mr. Lovell appeared suddenly before her.

"Miss Spencer! I am so glad to see you here. I was afraid you had not come after all. I have been looking for you and Miss Lorrimer everywhere, but the crush is so great I could not find you."

"Miss Lorrimer is with her aunt in the other room."

"Thank you. Thank you." He hesitated, and then said, "May I sit with you a moment. I have wanted the opportunity to speak with you."

"Please do," Katherine told him. She smiled at him as he took a seat beside her.

"You must know," he said with a rush, "how much I admire Miss Lorrimer. She is the sweetest, loveliest creature I have ever met. . . . Do you—do you think she could ever care for me?"

"She already does so, Mr. Lovell. I am very surprised that you cannot see it."

"Are you sure? I hoped so much . . . but I am so afraid—"

"I think *she* is afraid that you might find her Connexion with Trade unsuitable."

"So Richard told me. Of course that is nonsense! Why

it is *I*, Miss Spencer, who am quite unworthy of her. I have not the presumption to address her—a younger son with so little prospects, while *she* is an heiress. She will think—"

"Mr. Lovell," Katherine interrupted firmly. "Do you really care for Letty?"

"With all my heart."

"And you wish to marry her?"

"More than anything else in the world."

"And you want to make her happy?"

"Of course!"

"Then tell her so. Put aside all this nonsense of being unworthy of her and caring what others think. Speak to her before she comes to doubt you."

"You really think I should?"

"I do indeed."

He lifted his head. "You are quite right. Thank you." He looked at her earnestly. "I have wanted to apologise to you, Miss Spencer, for some time. Richard has told you everything, hasn't he—about Kielder and our wager."

"Yes, he has," she said, finding herself quite unable to be cross with him, he looked so repentant.

"It was my fault," he continued sheepishly. "*I* was the one who made the wager. Truth to say, I never thought he'd do it—I mean, go all the way to Northumberland!"

"I thought you knew him well."

He smiled. "He never did refuse a wager. Still, it was unforgiveable. We were foxed, you know—"

"There is no need to say anything more, Mr. Lovell. I have quite forgiven you. Besides, Lord Melvin lost the wager, after all."

"And you saved me fifty guineas, Miss Spencer, for which I am in your debt. And I shall be doubly so, since he will certainly lose the other wager, too."

"What other wager?"

"You know—the thirty guineas that he could not make

you fall in love with him before the month was out. I told him he hadn't a chance of winning. . . ." Mr. Lovell's voice trailed away. "He did tell you *everything?*"

Miss Spencer had gone very still. She looked down at her hands, which were clasped in her lap, and then said in a calm voice, "Of course, I had quite forgotten. As you say, he will certainly lose that one too. So you will be thirty guineas the richer, as well as your fifty." She stood up. "Please excuse me, Mr. Lovell. You will find Letty talking to some officers at the far end of the next room."

She quitted the anteroom. Mr. Lovell sat looking thoughtful for a moment.

"Where is Miss Spencer, David?"

Mr. Lovell, who by this time had reached a very unhappy conclusion, said in stricken tones, "I swear, I thought she knew, Richard. I thought you had told her everything."

The viscount said quietly, "Am I to understand by that, David, that you told her of our second wager?"

The other nodded miserably.

"Then you had better drink this. You look as though you need it."

Mr. Lovell took the proffered glass and drained the contents at one gulp. Then he said, dismayed, "But that was for Miss Spencer."

"I rather doubt," Lord Melvin said, "that she will return for it now."

Lady Mablethorpe was not sorry for the chance to be rid of the Northumberland nobody who had monopolised her most eligible guest. On learning that Miss Spencer had a headache and wished to go home, she lost no time in putting her carriage at her disposal and bid her farewell with a sigh of relief. Several of her friends with marriageable daughters had been seriously put out by the turn of events, which would not do at all.

Katherine despised herself for running away, and yet she knew she could not have stayed to face Lord Melvin. Mere anger would have spurred her to do so, but humiliation had had the contrary effect. So it had all been for another wager. The kiss, the tour of London, the clever flattery, the silver-tongued fatal charm had all been for the sake of winning thirty guineas! How cunningly he had played his cards, how subtly, how winningly—how *despicably*! And how could she have been so blind! Well, thank God for Mr. Lovell! He had saved her from complete humiliation—just in time. The wager was lost, as the one before it, and his lordship would shrug his shoulders, laugh, and then forget all about it.

Miss Spencer was awakened next morning early by Letty, who came bouncing into the room with a smile on her face as bright as the morning sun.

"Guess what, Kate! Guess what has happened!"

Katherine opened her eyes wearily. "Mr. Lovell has proposed and you have accepted."

"How did you guess?"

"It was not so very difficult. Oh, Letty, I am *so* pleased for you. I know you will be happy with him." She sat up and hugged Letty, who perched herself excitedly on the end of the bed.

"Of course he has not yet asked Papa, but he has quite overcome all that silly nonsense about my fortune. And he is not the least bit put off by my Connexion."

"I am very glad to hear it."

"Are you feeling better, Kate? You look very pale."

"Yes, thank you."

"What a pity you had to leave early from Lady Mablethorpe's. There was music and dancing, you know, later on, after you had gone."

"Was there?"

"Lord Melvin was very concerned about you."

"Letty, you will do me a great service if you will be so good as to refrain from ever mentioning that gentleman's name to me again."

"Oh dear! Are you angry with him again, Kate? Just as I was hoping . . . oh well, of course I shan't mention it if you would prefer not."

"I should very much prefer not." Katherine put her feet to the floor. "Letty, you will not mind if I return to Kielder as soon as possible?"

"*Must* you go? It seems such a pity, and I shall miss you."

"No you won't. You will have Mr. Lovell to look after you. And I should go back to Will."

"I have just thought of something, Kate. If you are really determined to go, then you will be able to speak to Papa about David. You will do that for me, won't you? Tell him that he is the most perfect man in the world! If Papa does not give his consent, I shall die!"

"Which would not help at all."

"So you will speak to Papa? You promise?"

"I promise."

"Dear Kate," Letty said seriously. "How I hope that one day you will find someone as nice as David, and be as happy as I."

"There is always Vernon. Do not forget him."

"Kate! You wouldn't . . . !"

"No, I shouldn't. Never fear. But, oh, how I long now to be back at Kielder!"

= 10 =

SIR WILLIAM SPENCER greeted his sister's arrival home with almost as much relief as she felt herself. The long journey by stagecoach had been gruelling, and by the time she reached Kielder she was almost too tired to think. The sight of the familiar outline of the castle against the sky had moved her to tears. It had never seemed more dear to her. Her brother's unusual enthusiasm at regaining her company she shrewdly attributed to his having been left in charge of Nurse. Indeed, it was not long before a string of grievances and grumbles came pouring out, of all the constraints and indignities he had had to endure in her absence.

"Gruel, Kate! *Gruel!* And *fish!* You know how I hate fish!"

"It is very good for you."

"Not if it makes me sick."

Boots thumped his tail in sympathy.

"Has Mr. Merryman been to give you your lessons?"

"*More* Latin and *more* Greek! What's the use of languages that nobody speaks anymore, I'd like to know?" The baronet looked thoroughly disgusted. "And Nurse wouldn't even let me go shooting with Fowler."

"She was quite right to forbid it."

"I went with Mr. Drew."

"That was different."

"I don't see why." Will looked up hopefully. "Is Mr. Drew coming back soon?"

She turned away. "No, he is not coming back. He is

never coming back, Will. He tore up Harry's voucher. He has given Kielder back to you."

"I told you he was nice. I always liked him. So did Nurse. I'm sorry he won't be coming back."

"*Will!*" Katherine cried, exasperated. "Is that all you can think about! Aren't you pleased that Kielder belongs to you again?"

"Oh, I never thought Mr. Drew would keep it. I always knew he'd give it back to us in the end. He told me as much, when we were out shooting. You didn't really think he'd take it from us, did you, Kate? Not Mr. Drew!"

"He's not Mr. Drew," Katherine said pettishly.

"Isn't he?"

"He only called himself that for a wager. His real name is Lord Melvin."

"Oh! Well, anyway it doesn't matter what he's called, does it? I still wish he'd come back and take me out shooting again."

It was not long before Mr. Webber called at the castle. As he entered the small parlour Katherine saw with a sinking heart that he had evidently decided to overlook all her past failings, and that once again she was deemed worthy of the honour of becoming mistress of Sudley Hall.

He beamed at her with approval and bowed low over her hand. "My dear Katherine, allow me to say what a pleasure it is to have you home again."

"Thank you, Vernon."

He wagged an admonitory finger. "Mind you, when I heard that you and Letitia had gone to London, without a word of warning, I was shocked and upset. It was very rash of you. Mama thought it most imprudent."

"Did she? Pray do apologise to Mrs. Webber for my having caused her alarm."

"Letitia, of course, is much inclined to recklessness

and unwise adventure. It was the discovery of that very trait that made me doubt her suitability."

"Suitability for what, Vernon?"

He looked a little flustered. "Why—er, to be—er, that is . . ."

"That is what, Vernon?"

"I confess, Katherine, that I did once consider asking Letitia to become my wife. But when I gave the matter more serious thought—for it is a serious matter, you know—I reached the conclusion that she would not do at all. Not at all. Sudley Hall needs an infinitely more sober and discreet mistress, someone who would appreciate the position and duties entailed. In short, someone such as yourself."

To her dismay he lowered himself clumsily onto one knee.

"Not *again*, Vernon!"

He groped for her hand, undeterred. "Will you do me the honour, Katherine, of becoming my wife?"

"Oh, dear!" She tugged at her hand. "I am very grateful for the offer, but I must decline. Do get up, Vernon!"

"You refuse me?"

"I am really quite unworthy, you see. I have told you so several times before, if you remember. Your mama—"

"You need not concern yourself about Mama, she is quite reconciled to the idea. And you need not worry about your lack of fortune—though such a thing would be very useful, there is no denying—"

"Despite your mother's reconciliation, I must still say no. I am exceedingly sorry, but I fear we should not suit at all, you and I. I should not be at all a good wife for you, Vernon. You would find me very *un*suitable. Besides, there is Will."

Mr. Webber, who had completely forgotten the existence of the fourteenth baronet, said bravely, "He would come and live at Sudley Hall, naturally. I daresay Mama would not mind too much. After all, you have no other home now."

"Yes, we do. We have Kielder. Mr. Drew gave it back to us. It belongs to Will and he could not leave it."

"*Gave* it back to you! How remarkably generous! I must say that I think it more than Harry deserved. Well, well."

"So you see, Vernon. It is hopeless. You will just have to find someone else. And do get up."

Mr. Webber, still on one knee, pondered deeply for a moment. He was inclined to think that Katherine was right, after all. He had had great difficulty in persuading his mother to approve this proposal in the first place, and he had quite forgotton to mention the problem of Will. And if the family still owned Kielder, that made matters worse. Far from being an asset, the old castle was nothing but a liability. He might even be prevailed upon to pay for its upkeep, and it was bad enough keeping up Sudley Hall. The more he thought about it, the wiser it seemed to choose instead a wife with some resources. He struggled to his feet.

"May I ask when you expect Letitia to return?"

"It is no use your thinking of her instead, Vernon. Letty is to be married to Mr. Lovell. Why don't you go to London yourself and find a bride? I recommend it."

"Really, Katherine!"

"Why not? People do, I believe. You may be fortunate and find a rich heiress who has no connexion other than with the very best."

He went away exhibiting all the hurt pride of the rejected suitor; Katherine did not know whether to laugh or cry when he had gone. It was sad somehow to think that he would never propose to her or Letty again. She hoped he *would* go to London and find, at last, the suitable mistress for Sudley Hall.

She did not forget her promise to Letty and, one

afternoon, summoned her courage to call on Mr. Lorrimer. He was in the vilest of humours. His gout was troubling him, and he barked at her like a bad-tempered old dog. He had never lost the brusque manners and speech of his background, but being accustomed to his ways she took no notice. She sat with him beside the blazing fire in the stifling heat of the grange, and eventually broached the subject of Mr. Lovell.

Mr. Lorrimer brandished his stick furiously. "Marry my daughter, eh? I'll kill him first! A younger son without a penny! I want better for her than that!"

She soothed him down and spoke calmly in praise of Mr. Lovell. When she had finished he grunted.

"You say he's a good lad?"

"Very. He will make Letty happy, I promise."

He glared at her. "Hmmph! We'll see then, we'll see. I make no promises. No promises at all." He raised his bushy eyebrows at her. "When are you going to get wed then? When's some knight going to storm that old castle of yours and carry you off? If I were thirty years younger, by God, I'd do it myself!"

She left him in better humour and already half resigned to the idea of Letty's engagement. He would rant and roar, she knew, and terrify poor Mr. Lovell out of his wits, but in the end he would give his consent.

After the grange, Kielder seemed cold and bleak. When they had finished supper Katherine set the chess pieces out on the board and she and Will sat down to play. But her mind refused to stay on the game. She could not concentrate. Unbidden images of London kept floating before her . . . the gardens at Westminster Abbey, the view across the Thames, the Drive in Hyde Park. Instead of sitting beside the fire at Kielder, she was suddenly standing in the Whispering Gallery of St. Paul's, listening to a voice reciting verse. . . .

The loss of her queen brought her temporarily to her

senses. Will, scenting victory, hunched himself fiercely over the board. The long-case clock ticked in the corner.

"Mr. Drew to see you, ma'am."

Purves had appeared suddenly at the door, and at first Katherine thought the butler's age and failing eyesight must have muddled him, until she saw the visitor who walked into the great hall. Will jumped up, scattering chessmen and thus ruining a rare chance of victory; Boots lurched to his feet and wagged his tail.

"Mr. Drew! Kate said you were never coming back."

"Did she? Then your sister was mistaken, Will."

"Are you going to take me out shooting again?"

"It is your shoot now. It is for *you* to take me out."

"Is it? Oh yes, I suppose it is. Thank you, sir, for giving Kielder back, by the way. I've nearly beaten Kate at chess, you know."

"Have you? That's very good."

"She wasn't paying attention properly. I took her queen and I was just going to put her king into check when you arrived. Look, Mr. Drew."

But to Will's disappointment it was his sister who was receiving attention. She had risen, and was standing as though turned to stone. He thought she looked very white, and wondered, fascinated, if she was about to be sick.

"It is not Mr. Drew, Will."

"Don't be silly, Kate. Of course it is! You can see it is! I *thought* he would come back. Oh!" Will clapped his hand over his mouth. "His *name*, you mean. I'd forgotten. It's really Lord something, isn't it? But I hope you won't mind, sir, if I go on calling you Mr. Drew sometimes, because I'm sure I shan't remember. Oh *no!*"

This *cri de coeur* came from him at the sight of Nurse descending the staircase with purposeful tread. He backed away, but she advanced relentlessly and seized his arm. "Time for bed, laddie." She prodded him in the back with her stick. As they passed Lord Melvin she paused for a moment and nodded approvingly. "I see you've come back for her then. Aye, I knew you would. You'll have a job persuading her, mind. She's a stubborn lass, but dinna pay any heed to her blethering. She'll give in in the end, if she knows what's good for her."

She nodded again and dragged her charge, who protested and wailed at each step, away and up the stairs.

Miss Spencer began to pick up the scattered chessmen distractedly. Since some of them had been knocked to the floor in her brother's excitement, she was obliged to hunt about on the carpet. The white king, however, could not be found.

"Is this what you are looking for, Kate?"

The soft voice and the use of her pet name almost disarmed her, but she collected herself, and stood and held out the box coolly. He dropped the missing piece into it and she snapped the lid shut.

"Why have you come here? For another wager? You have already lost two on my account. Isn't that enough? But then, I suppose eighty guineas is nothing to you!"

He removed the box from her grasp and set it down on the table beside them. Then he took her hands firmly in his.

"I have come to ask you to marry me, Kate. I should have done so in London, if you had not run away from me. I have been trying to make you fall in love with me ever since we met—but not for any wager! I have loved you from the moment I first saw you when I arrived here that evening. And I thought, in London, that at last you were beginning to care for me. Now I am sure of it."

"How can you be sure?" she said indignantly.

"Simple, my love. You would not have run away when you learned about the second wager if you had not cared. You would have been angry, but that is all." His grip tightened on her fingers. "In any case, Kate, I am tired of waiting. The battle is lost for you. No one is on your side anymore. Nurse, Will, Letty, David, Mrs. Jennings, and my father—especially my father—all think you should marry me. Even Boots does. Don't you, Boots?"

The spaniel raised his head and wagged his tail traitorously.

"You see," said Lord Melvin, pulling Miss Spencer relentlessly into his arms. "It is checkmate, Katherine of Kielder, and you may as well surrender!"

It was some moments later that a voice piped up interestedly from the gallery above. "Mr. Drew! I say, Mr. Drew! When you've married Kate, will you still come out shooting with me?"

The viscount did not look up or turn his head. "Go to bed, Will."

"Yes, sir. But—"

"At *once!*"

"Yes, sir—er, my *lord*, I mean. What *is* your name, sir, by the way?"

"Richard. You may call me that, Will. Since we are to be brothers-in-law."

"Thank you, sir." There was a pause. "Good night, Kate."

"Good night, Will."

This last answer sounded rather breathless.

"I always thought you would marry Mr. Drew, you know." Another pause. "You promise you *will* marry him now, won't you, Kate?"

"I—I promise, Will."

"Well," said the fourteenth Baronet Spencer and the owner of Kielder Castle, content at last. "*That's* all right then. Good night!"

If you have enjoyed this book and would like to receive details of other Walker Regency romances, please write to:

Regency Editor
Walker and Company
720 Fifth Avenue
New York, NY 10019